FRIENDSHIP MAGICIAN

MERCHANT MAGICIAN
BOOK 2

JOHN CHAMPAIGN

INDEPENDENTLY PUBLISHED

Dedicated, along with everything I do, to my beloved wife.

CONTENTS

1

———

My twenty-third birthday party was a lot like my brother's had been. He's the "Merchant Magician." You may have read his silly book a couple of years back. In it, he claims he saved the world in a way that no one can verify, which seems awfully sus to me. He gets grumpy when I tease him about it. He also worked out a business deal with a colony of dwarves up in Iceland that really impressed my father.

Our family, who have traded mystical goods and services for centuries, has a whole coming-of-age thing for everyone's twenty-third birthday. It was nice to see everyone, but honestly, I'd prefer talking to any of the guests privately instead of a big gala. I was making the rounds and had been chatting with Unexpected Gust On An Autumn Evening for the last few minutes.

I made a series of whistling noises and that got it chatting again for another few minutes. Unexpected Gust is an air elemental. I'd been working on learning their language over the last couple of years. Quite a bit of their socialization is sharing experiences, ideally awe-inspiring experiences.

Most of the time I talk about seeing Sequoia National Park or the Sistine Chapel and air elementals seemed pleased. Unexpected Gust had been talking all night about a whiff of a volcanic eruption from the other side of the world that it'd caught the scent of last week.

After it'd finished it's recollections, I delivered a story of my own I'd been preparing for the next time we talked. I told it about my torrid love affair with a werewolf named Mark Raphael in college. After I went into details that would make me blush if I'd said them in a human language, I talked about our bittersweet breakup. Unexpected Gust stood in stunned silence, digesting my story, which I'd learned meant it was a hit. Air elementals seemed to enjoy hearing about life experiences different from their own.

I moved over to join Drigrin, the minotaur, who was laughing with some finance bros near one of the bars. "That's all fine and well," said the minotaur, "but about that term sheet..."

"Term sheets!?!" Brad said in drunken exasperation. He looked at me and flicked his thumb at Drigrin, "The guy in the ugly mask is a real nerd. Let's do shots. Hooter shooters off the birthday girl!"

My eyes met Drigrin's. Centuries ago a masking spell was cast that let mundanes pretend not to see supernatural elements of the world around them. Drigrin is, most certainly, not a guy in an ugly mask. He's pretty patient and tough to ruffle though, luckily for this crew.

"Hooter shooters would be for a strip club where I worked," I said to Brad, meeting his eyes and smiling. "Since you're here trying to get money out of my wealthy family, you're the ones working. Why don't you take off your shirts, then tell my friend about that term sheet."

Brad stared at me, trying to make sense out of the situation, then hollered, took a shot, and started taking his shirt off. His bros followed suit. Drigrin rolled his eyes at my smirk as I turned to move on.

I was halfway across the room, headed towards Professor Youngblood, when my brother intercepted me with his buddy Umar.

"Why'd you get the finance bros riled up?" my brother asked. Umar fished out some appetizers from the large pile on his napkin.

"They got themselves riled up. Why don't you or dad just say no to them, so we can get rid of them. Brad asked me for a hooter shooter," I said.

My brother flushed and glanced over at the group. "We think there's a deal to be done with them, but that's pretty rude on your birthday. Are you okay turning the other cheek?"

"You got it boss," I said, feeling myself heat up. "Or is dad my boss these days? It's tough to keep track."

As my brother looked at me, judging my reaction, and trying to think of a response, Umar cut in. "Have you tried these meatballs? They're lamb. Delicious. You don't see lamb often these days..."

He looked back questioningly as my brother and I looked at him. Umar asked me, "Uhh, did I wish you a happy birthday yet?"

"Twice," I said flatly and, moving around the two, continued towards Professor Youngblood.

"... and within a couple of decades, vampirism could be eradicated," said Professor Youngblood, wrapping up his elevator pitch. Six graduate students were in a tight clump behind him talking quietly among themselves. "Ah, it looks like your father is about to say something," said the professor.

"Everyone, your attention please," my father began, projecting loudly throughout the room. Brad and the bros kept drinking and goofing around quietly behind Drigrin. "Thank you all so much for joining us on my daughter's twenty-third birthday." Applause echoed through the banquet room.

"Two years ago, I made what I consider to be the biggest mistake of my life," dad said to scattered chuckles around the room. "I sent my son on a walkabout to prove himself. He had to build a business whose value rivaled my own. We invoked a ritual to ensure that he couldn't use any resources in this endeavor. My hope was to instill confidence in my son and show all our business associates that they have nothing to worry about in the next generation."

"After passing with flying colors, my son ended up becoming my most dangerous and savvy rival." Chuckles again passed around the room. "Continuing to run his own operation instead of returning to the family business."

"My happiest moments in life have been running the family business with my son and daughter. I may not be perfect, but I'm smart enough not to make the same mistake twice. I'm happy to congratulate my daughter on her coming of age, and welcome her IMMEDIATELY into the family business as my full partner. I have the utmost confidence in her, which I'm sure you all share." With his toast complete, my father took a drink, which was mirrored around the room, then applause sounded again.

I made my way towards the stage, to my father's surprise. When I climbed up to join him, he gestured that the floor was mine, and stepped down onto the floor.

"*I don't know half of you half as well as I should like; and I like less than half of you half as well as you deserve,*" I began, getting scattered chuckles from the few people who recognized the Tolkien reference. Frank McCourt, a leprechaun my brother had had business dealings with looked visibly amused, while Sheena, my brother's fiancé, feigned irritation and wagged her finger at me.

"Thank you all for joining me on my twenty-third birthday and coming-of-age." I toasted those gathered and we all took a drink. "Two years ago when my father invoked the ritual for my brother's coming-of-age, I was shocked and disappointed by it. My brother had been working in the business, doing deals, since he was a boy and I felt that anything he needed to prove had long since been proven."

"I was surprised when, after he completed his 'quest', he was treated differently by everyone in our community. Even by our own family. He had done a good job haggling deals for my father before, but afterwards everyone considered him his own man. He'd changed from a star employee, or recipient of nepotism," this got some chuckles, "to a force unto himself."

"While my father has changed his mind about the value of undergoing this ritual, I still see it. Even this evening, while we're celebrating my supposed 'coming-of-age', I get treated as my father or brother's right-hand-woman, instead of a force unto myself." At this my father frowned and opened his mouth to say something.

"I have therefore contracted with the goddess Styx and made the same sacred oath that my father made on my brother's behalf. I will receive no assistance or inheritance from my family or our contacts, other than words of encouragement, until I have amassed a fortune of my own that rivals that of my father and my brother."

"*I regret to announce that this is the end. I am going now. I bid you all a very fond farewell. Goodbye.*"

And with that, I vanished from the party and found myself in a dark, urban environment. The stench of urine and garbage hit me. Walking out of the alleyway I'd appeared in, I looked up at a nighttime skyline at a high tower with a bulge near the top, which I recognized as the CN Tower.

Toronto.

2

I'd passed Dundas Square and was headed south on Yonge street. My brother liked to call it a poor man's Time Square. The Eaton Center was closed, but I figured I'd find somewhere to spend the night in the area. I'd almost gotten down to Front street when a dirty man suddenly jumped in front of me.

"Don't let me freeze out here tonight, sweetheart," he said as he leaned in close to me. The smell of B.O. and feces hit me.

Smiling, I said, "Sorry, I'm a little down on my luck tonight myself, friend." I held my hands up to show I wasn't carrying a purse or anything. "I literally don't have cent on me."

He leaned in close and grabbed my arm. His fingers dug in painfully and left streaks of grime, as his face contorted in rage. "I don't need you to be sorry. I just need twenty dollars. What have you got hidden away in that party dress, party girl?"

I shouted, "No!" as I twisted out of his grasp and cringed away from him. Taking advantage of his surprise, I dashed into the street and was almost hit by a car that braked hard to avoid running me over. The driver hit me with a sustained blast from his horn. Watching for other cars, I hurried across the street.

Looking over my shoulder, I saw the homeless man screaming as he made his way across the street following me. A neon sign on a well-lit restaurant identified it as "Fran's." I rushed over to it and slipped inside. The homeless man paced outside and occasionally beat on the window.

A hostess came over to me, took in my clothes and dirty arm and asked how many were in my party. After assuring her it was just me, she sat me at the counter of the 50's style diner. The waitress behind the counter gave me a menu and asked if I wanted coffee.

"Just a glass of water to start, please," I said. I looked at my filthy arm and thought about hitting the washroom. Instead, I studied the menu while I waited for my pounding heart to slow down. Glancing at the front window, I made eye contact with the man outside and he became agitated again and angrily said something that I couldn't hear.

"What can I get you, hun?" asked the waitress as she stopped on the other side of the counter.

"I'll be honest with you," I admitted. "I just came in because that guy outside was getting aggressive with me. I don't have any money. Would it be ok if I just sat here until he went away?"

Frowning at me, the waitress said, "You're welcome to hang out here as long as you want, IF you make a purchase. Head over to Union Station and hang out there if you aren't buying anything. This isn't a space for vagrants."

I eyed the angry man in the window and looked back at the waitress. Her frown deepened as I tried my best winning smile on her.

"I'm kind of afraid of the angry guy outside," I said. I glanced at my dirty arm. "Could I just wash up in the bathroom and I'll leave as soon as he's gone?"

"The bathroom's for paying customers," she said. "You'll have to leave if you aren't buying anything." I glanced uncomfortably at the entrance.

"Get her a coffee on me," the man next to me said. With a cloying smile he looked me over and said, "I'm always happy to help a damsel in distress. I'm Henry." He held out his hand.

Shaking his hand back, I introduced myself. "The nightlife is a little livelier than I planned for," I said. My heartbeat had gotten closer to normal, this was a more familiar danger. The waitress gave a snort of annoyance as she put a coffee cup in front of me and filled it up. "How do you take it, hun?" she asked coldly.

"Just black, thanks," I responded.

"You should get some calories into yourself whenever you have the chance," Henry advised. He winked at me, "Who knows what the evening has in store for you yet."

"Good advice," I agreed. "Double cream and sugar then, please. If you'll excuse me, I'm just going to clean up and I'll be right back." I felt Henry's stare on me as I made my way to the bathroom.

A few minutes later I returned. Henry was staring at me as I came back. I held up my clean arm and said, "Looking better already, thanks again." Sitting down, I sipped my coffee.

"Lovely," he said. He shifted closer to me on his bolted-down stool. "So how did you get yourself into such a predicament?"

I started relating the events at my party, but while I was explaining that my family had been dealers of occult goods and services for centuries he lost interest and cut me off.

"And what are you doing here in Toronto?" he asked.

"I'm here entirely unexpectedly, actually," I answered. "A number of times over the…"

He cut me off again and said, "Where are you staying?"

I looked at Henry appraisingly. I've had productive meetings with people who had a conversational red flag or two, but cutting me off repeatedly and rapidly changing the subject wasn't a good sign of anything to come. In my experience, people who do this are rushing to a specific place in the conversation, often something that's to their benefit. You'll see this with scammy salesmen or pick-up artist types.

My father and brother have a bad habit of criticizing bad behavior like this when they encounter it. They defend this by saying how can people improve if you don't point out mistakes they're making. My experience has been that criticizing people is a fatal mistake when trying to befriend someone. Whether they're in the right or the wrong, they'll never forgive you for the criticism.

Smiling at him, I said, "Why do you ask?"

Ignoring my question, he leered at me. "I think you should come home with me tonight," he said, leaning closer yet. The waitress, sensing the direction the conversation was taking had moved away behind the counter and was watching from a distance.

"Well, that is certainly flattering," I said, smiling, then slipping off the stool. "And I really appreciate the coffee, but I should probably be moving on." He grabbed for my arm and I managed to slip out of reach from him.

What is up with Canadian guys and grabbing arms?

After missing me, he started to fall forward and caught himself on my (recently vacated) stool. I headed for the door quickly, looking outside for the panhandler from earlier. Seeing no sign of him, I exited and headed south toward Union Station. Henry shouted after me, "Hey, I bought you a coffee, you owe me," but I kept moving.

LOOKING at the departure and arrivals board, I saw that it was just after 3 am and that buses would be leaving soon for Thunder Bay and Montreal. A figure silently settled into the seat next to me. I looked over to see my brother sitting there eyeing me.

"So you've made your point, we're all suitably impressed and/or chagrined," he said, looking neither impressed nor chagrined. "What is it going to take to bring you home? I can transfer 51% of my operations to you or dad can transfer 73% of his to you. Either way, we're both willing to call you boss."

"Ah," I said, looking him over. "The payoff. I forget, did you accept the payoff when dad offered it to you?"

"This isn't a game," he said, getting annoyed. "Where are you anyways?" He looked around. "Chicago?"

"Toronto," I corrected. "I've already made a couple of friends on my way to the station. How did you get here anyways?"

He looked at the bruise that had formed on my arm and frowned. "One of the telepaths connected us, I'm not actually here. Anybody around you probably thinks you're talking to yourself. I don't get what you're after here. What do you want?"

"Ha ha, I'm the lucky recipient of one of your famous deals?" I said. "You and dad have never understood what I do."

"You're great at what you do. Everyone loves you. You maintain important relationships with the people we do business with. We're willing to give you whatever you want to keep doing it," he said. He gave me a pleading look.

"Ok, two years ago, what was the most important deal you did?" I asked.

"Other than saving the world, which you mock me about every time it comes up?" he said.

"Yes, other than the fantastic adventure that no one experienced other than you," I said.

"I guess that'd be the deal with the dwarves," he said thoughtfully.

I said, "I'll be sure to tell Sheena that that ranks above getting her to date you."

With a grimace he said, "Please don't tell her that. She'll never let it go."

"She already has a lot of stuff she never lets go," I said.

"Yeah, but she doesn't need new material," he said.

"Ok, let's talk about the dwarves. You view it as this magnificent deal where a bunch of things got loaded up on both sides of a scale and magically you transformed it into something where both sides got many times as much value as what they'd given up, right?" I said.

"Right," he agreed.

"That wasn't the important part of that transaction. Dwarves were difficult to interact with. You won over Granite. The friendship that you formed with him is the basis of any bargains you've made. The relationships I create, maintain, and grow are the most valuable parts of our business. And I'm going to prove that to you, dad, and everyone else," I said.

"You're arguing semantics here," he said. "For the sake of

argument, let's say I'm convinced. You're the friendship magician. Come back home."

"No," I said. "Because you aren't convinced. But you will be. Go tell dad that you tried your best, but there's no convincing me."

After a last long look, my brother disappeared with a flicker. I noticed the people around me were watching me out of the corners of their eyes.

As the board changed to show 6 am, I yawned and got up. Walking back up along Yonge Street, I headed back towards the Eaton Center. The city was getting going in the dawn and the rougher element from last night had retreated to wherever they spend their days.

Getting to the City Hall library branch, I was disappointed to see that it didn't open until 10 am. I wandered to the Eaton Center, intending to hang around the food court, and found they didn't open until 10 am either.

"Lazy Toronto folk," I thought as I continued north along Yonge Street. I found a congee restaurant and a Middle Eastern restaurant, but neither opened until quite a bit later. I entered the lobby of the Chelsea Hotel and saw their espresso bar was hopping with people getting ready to start their day. I hung around for a while, hoping for a break in the crowd for a chance to talk to one of the workers, but it seemed to be going pretty steady. I was about to leave when one of the bellboys came up next to me and said, "Anything I can help you with, miss?" with an Eastern European accent of some sort.

"This is kind of embarrassing, and I'm happy to leave if you're here to kick me out, but I was going to ask the workers if I could wash some dishes or do some work for them in exchange for a coffee and a pastry," I said. Seeing his unreadable expression, my embarrassment grew. "Sorry, please ignore me. I should be going." I started moving towards the front entrance.

"No, wait, stay here," he said and walked over to an employee-only doorway. A few minutes later he returned and handed me a brown paper bag. Looking inside, I saw a packed lunch.

"I can't take your lunch," I said, flushing red.

"I think you need it more than I do today. I really insist," he said.

Thanking him repeatedly, I left the hotel and ate the gifted food as I made my way back to the library and waited for them to open.

JOB WANTED - LET ME DO THE DIRTY WORK.

I offer cleaning services around Toronto (anywhere reachable by public transit).

Whether you are moving in or moving out, I'll clean so you don't have to.

You provide the cleaning supplies, I supply the elbow grease. $20 / hour cash paid at completion of work

the.friendship.magician@gmail.com

I POSTED the ad to Craigslist, Kijiji, and Facebook Marketplace with my newly created email address. I had booked three appointments for later in the day and was waiting for any additional emails when one of the library workers approached me.

"I'm sorry, but you've been on the computer for an hour now. We're going to have to ask you to wrap up whatever you're doing to give other patrons a chance to use the equipment," she said.

I looked in confusion at the empty computers surrounding us. "So, even though there are computers available for anyone else to use, you want me to get off of this one?" I asked.

"Yes," she said, giving me a blank expression. "It's our policy."

"Fair enough," I said and logged off. I discretely tucked the cleaning job information that I'd written on slips of paper into my bra.

Arriving at the first cleaning job, the resident looked doubtfully at my dress and explained that she was moving out and needed the unit cleaned in order to get her security deposit back. She offered to let me wear some of her clean workout clothes, which I accepted, and two hours later she gave me $50 and let me keep the clothes.

The owner at the second appointment didn't answer the door when I knocked. After waiting around for fifteen minutes and not finding anyone, I headed to another library branch and spent another hour on the computers. I got the addresses of a few women's shelters and spent some time looking up the occult communities in Toronto. I also arranged five more cleaning appointments for the next day.

I bought a Presto card for public transit and put some money on it to get to the third appointment. The young man who opened the door smirked at my oversized clothes and the dress I was carrying but offered me a bag to put it all in and paid me $30 after I'd cleaned for an hour and a half for him. He sat the entire time watching me and talking about his new girlfriend who he wanted to impress with his clean place.

IN A BED in the dorm at the women's shelter, I had my tote bag under the covers of the bed I was in. Fifteen women in other bunks in the large room made varying amounts of noise as they slept or tried to fall asleep. I thought about my schedule for tomorrow and fell asleep thinking about the best way to get around to each job.

3

The shelter's pastor finished a fifteen-minute lecture about how open-minded Christians are and I exchanged looks with the bored women at my table. Sheets were removed from the breakfast food, revealing stale donuts (again) and carafes of coffee. A few of the newer women rushed over to the breakfast, while those of us who had been here for a while waited patiently, knowing that the stale donuts wouldn't all get gobbled up.

"What are you all planning to do today?" asked Shannon.

I said, "Five cleaning jobs. A couple of them are big ones if anyone wants to join me." None of the women gave any indication of being interested in joining me.

"You really need to get an education or learn a trade," said Shannon. "Cleaning isn't an appropriate life-long career path for an ambitious young woman."

"How's your fancy degree helping you get out of here?" asked Tara. The rest of us braced ourselves for a repeat of the same argument they'd had the last two mornings.

"I went on three interviews last week," said Shannon. "When I get out of here, I'm not going to end up right back here like the rest of you will. You all haven't had the misfortunes in your life I have. Chronic pain syndrome isn't something..."

Beth cut her off. "We don't compare misfortunes here Shannon. We've gone over this before." Shannon gave her a dirty look. Seeing the women at the serving table thin out, Janet got up and walked over to it.

"I'm not really looking for a long-term career, just some fast cash," I said. "I actually have an undergraduate degree in communications..."

"But you can't get your paperwork," Tara said, cutting me off. "We've heard it before."

"I've been researching groups in Toronto to make contact with," I said, dropping the conversational thread about my credentials. "There's an orc horde that operates up in Markham that..."

"We don't live in fantasy worlds here," Beth cut me off. Janet returned with a pile of donuts and coffees for herself and Beth. The rest of us went up to the table to grab a coffee.

"What are your plans for the day?" I asked Tara.

Glowering at me, she said, "Don't get into my business, fish."

Smiling at her I said, "Isn't that a term for new people in a men's prison? Does it really apply to me?"

Darkening further, Tara said, "Keep it up if you want me to hurt you."

Shutting up, I pulled a thermos I'd bought yesterday out of my bag. Holding it up to one of the women behind the table I said, "Do you mind if I fill up my thermos with coffee for the day?"

She looked at me blankly for a few seconds, then shrugged. I filled it up.

"So HOW WOULD you work with this Orc horde?" asked Rasmus, the bellboy from the Chelsea Hotel who had given me his lunch. Sipping at the coffee I'd poured into his cup he grimaced. "This coffee, it's not good!"

"Yeah, it's terrible," I agreed. "The price is right though. They'd expect me to defeat their weakest member in one-on-one combat."

"Are you a mystical badass? Could you beat him?" said Rasmus.

I said, "I took judo in junior high. I went to one session and then dropped out. I don't think I could defeat ANY orc in one-on-one combat. Personal combat is kind of their thing. They're all devoted to it. Basically, they're green Klingons."

"What are your other options?" he asked, missing my Star Trek reference.

"There's an elven court in High Park," I said. "None of the merchant families have much contact with them. They're pretty traditional and feudal, and aren't big on trade missions. They also really hold grudges and have grievances of some sort against most of the merchant families."

"Hmm," he said. "Any other options?"

"There are giant rats that are starting to be a problem in the PATH Underground Shopping Mall," I said. "Newbie adventurers are usually the solution to problems like that. Toronto doesn't have an adventurer's guild, so I'd have to go to Ottawa or Quebec City to recruit a party to take care of them. They'd want some sort of reward before they'd accept the quest, so I'd have to figure that out too."

"You're quite open-minded about all this," I said, observing him closely. "The women at my shelter won't let me talk about any of this."

"My grandfather was cursed by a witch, then had the curse lifted by another witch, when I was a boy," he said. "I know there are things out there in the unseen world."

"I could help you see it, if you're interested," I offered.

"No, thanks," he said. "If kobolds or warlocks are staying at the hotel, I don't want to offend them by staring at them. I'm happy to just treat them like any other guest."

"By the way," he continued. "I heard about a rooming house-type affair on Spadina that you might be interested in. They're furnished, shared access to kitchen space and bathrooms, and you rent a bed in a shared room. Usually, they like to rent to U of T students, but they have some beds that weren't rented and they don't expect to get a student now that the school term has started." He handed me a slip of paper. "Here's the owner's daughter's contact information. Right in the heart of Chinatown."

"I'll check it out, thanks!" I said.

I STOOD under one of the sakura trees and sang the song of elven greeting for the third time. I had found a forest green pantsuit at Value Village that seemed appropriate for the meeting. A number of people relaxing in the park looked at me in confusion as they strolled or rode past where I was. I took a few breaths and was preparing for my fourth rendition when I heard a high-pitched voice behind me.

"Your song of welcome is heard and understood," the elf

said. "Please state your business with the elven court of the regent Ellisar, long may they rule."

Turning around I saw a small creature, about three and a half feet tall. He wore a green outfit that looked vaguely like a cartoonish Robin Hood costume. A small bow and quiver full of arrows was slung over one of his shoulders. He looked at me with boredom.

"Well met, friend elf," I began. "Thank you for answering my song."

"I couldn't very well ignore it. It's echoing throughout the realm, annoying everyone. They sent me to get you to stop singing," he said.

"Ahh," I said. "Sorry about that." I tried to give him a smile.

"You're from one of those merchant houses, aren't you?" he asked, examining me closely. "The last time we had a visit from a merchant house, it was Sayyid Umar Imran about a year ago."

"I know Umar!" I said.

"He called me a Peter Pan looking mother fucker," finished the elf.

"He's a friend of my brother's. I don't really like him that much. He's rude," I said.

"Your brother..." the elf said, looking at me appraisingly. "In that case, your great grandfather came here 73 years ago, called the Regent Ellisar a 'jolly little fellow', and never delivered the seven gallons of molasses he promised us. We have no interest in you, your family, or your ill-mannered, dishonest trading house." He began to turn away from me.

"I'm no longer a part of that trading house," I said. He paused. "I invoked a ritual with the goddess Styx making me independent of them."

"Well then, emissary of a new 'trading house' of one. What do you want from us?" he asked.

"I'm trying to establish myself, starting from nothing," I explained. "I'm hoping to talk to you and see if there's anything I can exchange with you to help get me started."

"We have no enthusiasm for this strange barter game that consumes humans," said the elf dismissively. "Beg somewhere else."

"If there're no deals we can do, perhaps I could work for the court. I have a variety of skills I'm sure you'd find useful," I said.

Turning back to me, the elf asked, "You wish to pledge lifelong fealty and servitude to our court?"

"Well, more of a temporary fealty and servitude. In exchange for wages," I said.

"You have a high opinion of yourself that you'd think we'd be so desperate for your labors until a better offer comes your way. I grow weary of your peddler jibber jabber. Begone, and trouble us no more," he said.

"Before I leave, let me please just leave you with a gift, for you and your court," I said. I dug through my bag and pulled out multiple containers. The elf looked at the bags suspiciously.

Pulling out the first, I opened the container and held it out to him. "These are 'pastel de nata'. They're a Portuguese egg custard tart pastry. They're from Nova Era Bakery, here in Toronto, but you may have seen them being made a few seasons ago on 'The Great British Bake Off'."

Sniffing, the elf said, "I prefer elven food, thank you very much."

"Are you sure?" I asked. "They're delicious and I have a bunch of other pastries here. Maybe you'd like a Korean walnut pastry better?"

"Fine, fine," said the elf. Taking the tart from me he sniffed it again. "If this is what it takes to get you to go away." He bit into the pastry and the angry look on his face dissolved.

"Ahh," he said. "There's a lot going on there." He took another bigger bite. After he finished chewing it and swallowed, he said "Let's see what else you've got in that bag."

4

"So how do I add music to it?" asked the elf Vaeril.

"You can't with the desktop version of it," I explained. "You either have to embed the sounds you want with the video, then upload it to their site, or you can select a sound separately with the app."

"TikTok is my least favorite social media," they complained, frowning. They had explained to me, contrary to my original assumption, that they weren't male and corrected my usage of 'he'.

"I should get going if I'm going to hit the bakeries before they close," I said. "Will you be ok on your own for a few hours."

"Sure, sure," they said absently. "Take my pet with you. It needs to learn how to do the bakery run in case you leave."

"The mundanes don't view your pet as a person," I said. "They think it's an unusual dog breed when I bring it."

"Well, bring it anyways. It can learn the route and how to make purchases if nothing else," they said.

"Speaking of which," I began. "You know how humans like to barter things? I've spent all my money and don't have anything left to buy pastries with. I can't pay for my bed at the rooming house either. If you don't have any money for me, I'm going to have to go back to cleaning for most of the day to get more cash."

Stopping what he was doing, Vaeril turned to look at me. "But I need you here. We're going to do sound editing soon."

"Do you have anything I can trade for money?" I asked. "I could sell it, then use the money I get from the sale to pay for the pastries and my rent."

"Do humans buy mithril?" Vaeril asked.

"No, they don't know what it is," I said.

"Adamantium? Dilithium? Etherium? Katchin? Octiron?" they suggested.

"None of those," I said.

"They must like unobtainium," they said. "That's hard to get."

"Not even that. I could find buyers for any of that, but it would take me a bit of work," I said.

"Do humans like silver?" they asked.

"Yes," I said with a smile. "Silver will work."

"How many tons do you need?" they asked.

"Six ounces or a single pound would be fine for today," I said.

"Pet," they called. The squirrel creature ran over and crouched in front of the elf attentively. Its buck teeth quivered in anticipation.

"Fetch three pounds of silver and go with our friend to exchange it for money. Then go with her and buy pastries. Pay close attention, you may have to do this without her in the future. Be diligent and learn well," they instructed.

"Yes, parent. I obey," it said, chittering at the end of the sentence.

I ATE a few more kernels of popcorn as the end credits of 'House of the Dragon' played. "What did you think?" I asked.

"When are we going to see the Children of the Forest?" asked Vaeril. "They were hardly in 'Game of Thrones', and we haven't seen them in the first season of 'HotD' at all yet."

"Yeah, the focus has definitely been more on human societies in both shows," I agreed.

"No squirrels," said Vaeril's pet.

"Quiet pet, we're talking," said Vaeril and affectionately pat the creature's head.

"You never told me your pet's name," I said.

"Pets don't get names until they're fully grown," Vaeril explained.

"He's pretty big, how much larger is he going to get?" I asked.

"It, not he," Vaeril corrected. "Its size won't change much, but it's not a full-grown elf yet. It'll get a name when it becomes one."

"Huh?" I asked, confused.

"Huh, what?" they asked, amused.

"It's obviously a he. I'm happy to use 'It' if that's its preferred pronoun though," I said. "Please tell me if I'm offending you, that's the last thing I'd want to do."

Vaeril laughed. "It isn't a preferred pronoun. You're right that my pet was a male, but it's transitioning beyond gender. Eventually, you won't be able to tell which gender it was originally and it'll be completely androgynous, like me."

"No offense, but you aren't completely androgynous. You definitely lean masculine," I observed.

Laughing harder, Vaeril fell sideways on the couch. "That's quite a trick, as I was originally female."

"Really?" I asked "And why did you stop?"

"Because I grew up, I stopped being female when I stopped being a deer," they explained.

"A deer?" I asked shocked. "You were originally a deer?"

"Up until about 130 years ago," they explained.

"Are elves different, based on the animals they were before they 'grew up'?" I asked.

"No, we all end up in the same place. We become whatever elf we're meant to be. You wouldn't be able to guess what animal an elf was growing up if they wouldn't tell you," they said.

"The regent must have been a lion or a wolf or something though, right?" I observed. "Maybe an eagle? Something regal."

Laughing again, Vaeril said, "They were a carp in the region now known as China, before it was China."

"Wild," I said. "I'm not going to start turning into an elf, am I?"

"No," Vaeril said. "Sentient species can't be raised. Honestly, we look at other sentients as somewhat defective pets that can't be trained properly."

"So, I'm like a dog that can't be housebroken," I asked seriously.

"Exactly," agreed the elf.

Laughing I said, "Don't ever make that comparison to another non-elf! They'll be very offended."

VAERIL'S PET put some pastries into a bag and handed it to

the elf Gantar. "Good pet," the elf said, taking the bag. "Your owner is a real piece of shit, by the way."

"Oh, I'm sorry, you don't get along with Vaeril?" I asked.

"I was sick about eighty years back, Vaeril knew, and never sent food or well wishes the whole time," said Gantar. "When I told them how rude they were, they told me I'm too sensitive. Me! Too sensitive!"

"When they were a young elf, about 150 years back..." they continued.

"Vaeril has only been an elf for 130 years," I said.

"One hundred and thirty years back then, they were learning archery and they accidentally hit my house with three arrows. They didn't fix the damage until fifteen years or so ago. Over a century with arrow damage to my house!" Gantar said.

"Then, when I told them they'd taken too long to repair the damage, they called me a human!" Gantar said.

"I suppose there might be worse things to be called," I said with a grin.

"No offense of course," Gantar said. "I like humans as much as the next person. I'm friends with a human. Some young lad. He explained how tipping works the other day to me."

"That was me!" I said with a laugh. "I'm glad we're friends, though. Also, I'm a girl, not a boy."

"Yes, well. Maybe I'll save the other twenty-seven times Vaeril mistreated me for another day," they said. Pulling out a beautifully worked silver bracelet, they held it out to me. "Thank you for your hard work. I want you to have this tip."

"It's beautiful! But a silver bracelet is too much for a tip. You'd normally just give a few dollars," I objected.

"I don't have any dollars, so this is what you're getting," Gantar said and pushed the bracelet towards me again.

Putting it on, I held it up for the elf to see. "Thanks so much!"

"Thanks so much!" chittered Vaeril's pet, echoing me.

"Good soon-to-be gender-neutral, proto-elf," I said and pet its head. "Very polite."

VAERIL LOOKED AT ME SKEPTICALLY. "Those don't look like any formal human clothes I've ever seen before. You look like a human trying to disguise yourself as a dog."

"A dog?" I said, trying my best to look innocent. "I don't know what you're talking about. This is the current fashion in human formal wear."

I gestured over my outfit, which was a Halloween dog costume, complete with a dog's nose, whiskers, and a pair of floppy ears.

"You're the human, I suppose you'd know best," they said, looking pensively at the floppy ears.

I thought back to my conversation with the elf Revalor. They hadn't understood my idea at first, but when I told them about Vaeril comparing other sentient species to dogs they had laughed uncontrollably for minutes and insisted that I had to do it at the Midsummer tribunal.

I stressed repeatedly that I didn't want to embarrass Vaeril, but they'd assured me it would bring great honor to have a vassal perform such a jest. All my research had supported this.

Pavilions had been set up in a massive circle, each elf on their own, a distinct distance from one another.

"This is the first time I've seen elves with one another," I said.

"These elves are a bunch of garbage individuals. Real

trash," Vaeril observed with a sneer and looked angry. "Do you know how late the regent was starting the tribunal sixty-seven years ago? Three hours and twenty-four minutes. And we all just sat here waiting for them. So obnoxious!"

"Why don't you all leave and live somewhere else?" I asked.

"Without other elves?" they asked aghast. "That would be so lonely."

"But you all seem to dislike each other so much," I observed.

"Try spending centuries with a small group of people and see how well you like them at the end of it," Vaeril said. "Humans are lucky they get to die after eighty years or so. I'd had my fill of this crew after eighty years, let me tell you that!"

"If elves live forever and you train new elves, what happens when there are too many elves to meet up for a tribunal?" I asked.

"That's when an elven court splits in half and one group moves somewhere new," Vaeril explained. "I've never been through that, but the group here formed when a court in America was leaving during their revolution. They decided to use the move as an opportunity to split in half. One group came here and the other ended up in Vancouver. I think the area the court occupies is called Stanley Park now.

"Attention please, attention everyone," called out the regent.

Leaning towards me, Vaeril whispered, "Three minutes late," and gave me a knowing look.

"We would like to start by welcoming our new subjects," the regent declared. "Feyrith has taken into service a kobold, as has Theodmon. Mitalar has adopted a pet, an adorable budgie. Anfalen has taken a troll into service. Vaeril has a human, although it's been explained to me that this is a temporary service arrangement. We weren't aware that was something an elf could do, but apparently, the younger generation does things differently."

A few scattered chuckles greeted this and a large number of dark looks fixated on the regent. "Welcome to our court, our new vassals. We are certain you will impress us with your loyalty and hard work."

That's my cue, I thought to myself and dropped to my hands and knees. Barking repeatedly, I began pulling at Vaeril's pants with my teeth. I crawled around the pavilion jumping and barking.

"Whatever are you doing?" asked Vaeril perplexed. I felt the eyes of all the elves from the court on me.

On the other side of the gathering I heard howls of laughter coming from Revalor and gasped explanations between fits of laughter. *Gotta commit to the bit* I thought and put my on hands on Vaeril's chest and started licking their face.

Pulling away from me, the elf said, "I'm very fond of you, but I'm not comfortable with you licking me."

Laughter spread throughout the tribunal as perplexed elves struggled to hear the explanation then joined the laughter once they'd heard. When the elf two pavilions down was passing along what they'd heard, Vaeril finally got the joke and joined in the laughing. "This is all because I compared you to a dog? Come here then, you beast," and started rubbing my belly.

Twenty minutes later things had calmed down and the regent announced, "Well, that was a jolly good spoof from Vaeril. We commend them. Perhaps they will send their amusing new 'pet' to me to admire up close."

The elves' faces were happier through the rest of the

tribunal and Vaeril kept looking at me out of the corner of their eye and chuckling.

Bowing low, I offered the package to the regent. The tiny monarch accepted them daintily and looked at the packages.

"It's an assortment of candy from America, your majesty," I explained. "There are PayDays, Almond Joys and Mounds, Butterfingers, and M&Ms there. Vaeril explained to me that this court was formed when you came to Canada during the revolutionary war."

"Poor King Georgie," the regent said, with a sad face. "I met him you know. Very sweet boy. Has the new girl reclaimed America yet?"

"New girl?" I asked.

"Beth," the regent said.

"Queen Elizabeth the 2nd?" I asked. "She just passed away, unfortunately. The new king is her son Charles."

"Passed away!" the regent gasped. "Taken in her prime..."

"She was ninety-six years old your majesty," I explained.

"Such a tragedy, losing a youngster like that. I met her you know. During her royal visit seventy years ago. Before she was queen. I can't understand why they let these young people take the throne then die so quickly. Doesn't make any sense. Also, why hasn't she retaken America? She had seventy years on the throne to do so!" the regent said.

"I don't really know, your majesty," I admitted.

"We thank you for the thoughtful confectionaries. They will be a nice accompaniment to my drink of morning dew every dawn," the regent proclaimed. "We have been enjoying the technological devices you have set up for us. The old diversions like fox hunting have fallen out of favor, and it's so hard to find amusements. I have begun watching 'Downton Abbey' and am amazed at all the modern notions!"

"Yes, I enjoyed that myself," I said. "The Dowager Countess is my favorite character."

"Yes, she's a feisty, girlish thing, isn't she?" the regent said. "Ahh, to be young again."

"YOU'RE LEAVING?" asked Vaeril, shocked. "But you *JUST* got here. When did you start working for us? Yesterday? The day before?"

"It's been months," I said. "And I'm going to miss you too."

"I thought you'd be here for at least a decade or two. Why don't you give it another five years and see how you're feeling then?" they suggested.

"Your pet has learned to do the grocery run, selling silver, and most of the computer work I've been doing," I said. "It's even gotten quite good at managing the kobolds. It'll be able to handle all of that as well as I have."

"But you're leaving me with all these asshole elves!" they protested.

"Come with me, if you want," I suggested. "It'll be an adventure!"

"I can't leave the court," they said, sadly.

I said, "Not even for a holiday?"

After a pause, they said, "I don't think so."

"We'll stay in touch by email, let me know if you change

your mind," I assured them. "And I'll come to visit every time I'm in Toronto."

"Where are you going next?" they asked.

"I'm dropping off some elven food for a friend of mine in the city. He gave me his lunch when I was first in town, so I'm going to treat him and his family to an elven feast as a thank you," I said. "Then the regent has asked me to deliver some gifts to the Stanley Park court. After that, I found out about a mystic named Sohvi in northern Finland that I'm going to look into and see if she can help guide me."

"That's kind of you, to help the regent like that, even though you're ending your vassalage," they said morosely. "Theodred went on a trip once. They said they'd write me, but they didn't. That fucker."

"I will write you," I assured them. "And maybe you could patch things up with Theodred. That doesn't seem like the most unforgivable thing."

"Oh, that's not the half of it. Let me tell you everything they've done to me over the years!" Vaeril said, cheering up.

Holding up my hand, I said, "Next time I'm here!"

5

"But, this is simply the perfect solution," Mrs. Silverberg said over the phone. "Mrs. Imran makes you a vice-president, you marry Umar. She's very impressed by your qualifications and predicts you have a bright future in their family. She even said that you're almost good enough for her son! That's high praise from Mrs. Imran."

Lying back in the queen sized bed in my Helsinki Airbnb I rubbed my hand across my face. "I actually know Umar fairly well. He's a friend of my brother's. He really offended the High Park elven court in Toronto, you know."

"What did he do?" said Mrs. Silverberg, excited for some gossip.

"Pardon my language," I prefaced my news, "But he called their liaison Vaeril a 'Peter Pan looking mother fucker' apparently."

"Well, there you go, that's exactly the reason he needs a wife. Save him from himself and help guide him through situations like that," she said, pushing her case.

"I'm really sorry Mrs. Silverberg, but I'm building my

own enterprise, my own way. My father and brother would both love to have me work for them. I'm really not looking for a job, or a husband, right now," I said.

"Young people these days," she said in exasperation. "I had the perfect match for your brother, and he was just as stubborn. Is he still planning to marry that cultist?"

"Yeah, Sheena's great," I said.

"A cultist though!" she said. "I could have done better than that. Do you think he'd be open to meeting a nice enchanter I know before he walks down the aisle? Also, I've been looking to hire someone to handle my house's client relations. We have double the customer service representatives that your father has, so it'd definitely be a more prominent position. When can we bring you on?"

"I'll tell him to get in touch with you about the enchanter. I really appreciate the offer but, as I said, I'm really not looking for a job," I said. "Plus, you're offering me the position based on what you know of me before I began the ritual. Accepting a job from you would violate it."

"Oh, pish-posh. We can get Styx to come around to our way of thinking," the older woman said. "Do you know anything about Silvana Ureña? She's turning fifteen in a couple of months..."

HIKING ALONG THE ROUGH ROAD, I kept searching for the mystic Sohvi in the area I'd been told she frequents. It was my third day of searching and I was past impatience and starting to enjoy the ability to hike, guilt free, for days at a time.

My phone made a noise for my attention and I saw that an email from my father had arrived. I leaned on my walking stick and skimmed the message. It was another attempt from him to convince me to give up on this and come back home.

A breeze caught my hat and I had to grab it before it blew away.

Apparently business with the air elementals had come to a halt and Drigrin was irate because he wanted to move his business over to me, but couldn't do so without violating the ritual. My father had wrapped up a couple of deals with the finance bros, but he was getting frustrated with them now that he was dealing with them directly. Reading between the lines, I got the impression they'd twisted his arm to go to a strip club and he was particularly grumpy about that.

I had to crouch down as I was buffeted by the wind. I hunched over the phone and glanced over the other new messages. I marked most of the ones I knew I could ignore as 'read' without opening them.

A loud crash caught my attention and I looked up to see a violent storm heading my way from the east. In front of the thunderhead was a figure riding a white horse with large wings. Underneath them, a tree had splintered and caught fire, billowing smoke.

Closing towards me, another bolt of lightning shot past the rider, unsettling the mount and caused it to abruptly drop twenty or thirty feet. The bolt shattered another tree and added more smoke into the air. The rider seemed to have lost their seat when the mount arrested their descent and now swayed from side-to-side, barely hanging on. The flying horse was thrown off by the rider's erratic movements and plummeted again briefly before catching himself in an updraft.

They had gotten close enough that I could make out the

figure was a woman, fully covered in mail armor, high-lighted by fur. A horned helmet was on her head and she carried a spear.

As her pegasus came in for a landing, a gust caught them and she lurched to one side. Unbalanced, the mount hit the ground at an angle and was thrown sideways, throwing the valkyrie off. The two of them separated, tumbled along the ground, carving grooves into the turf and came to rest.

The warrior woman's helmet had been knocked off, and dirt and grass clung to her mail as she stood up. She picked up her spear and helmet and a few larger clumps of dirt and grass fell off of her. She looked expectantly in front of her, but didn't turn around until I said, "Hello?"

"Ah, Siegfried, it warms my heart to see you, my friend," she said. "You look so hale and youthful! But where is your sword?" The winged horse had righted itself and was climbing back to its feet. The valkyrie herself was the most muscular person I'd seen in my life. Every part of her body was enormous muscles, which was stuffed into her armor and bulged out of every gap in it.

"I'm not Siegfried, but are you ok? That was a nasty fall. Is your mount ok?" I asked. The storm raged around us. No rain fell, but occasionally bolts of lightning, accompanied by thunder, would smash the trees around us.

"Not Siegfried? Now is no time for jokes. I'm here to guide you on your quest," she said. Cleaning out her helmet, she started trying to pull it back onto her head. Her muscular head wouldn't fit, and ultimately she needed to pound the helmet with her fists to jam it on. The winged horse started nibbling on grass, ignoring us, as she did this.

"Is your pegasus ok?" I asked. "Are we safe in this storm?"

"He isn't 'a pegasus'," she corrected. "Pegasus was the name of a specific creature in Greek mythology, not a species. He's a winged stallion." The winged stallion gave the valkyrie an annoyed look.

I asked, "What's his name?"

"Pegasus," she said. "Named AFTER the Greek creature. This isn't Pegasus himself. Well, he is I suppose. But not THE Pegasus. If you follow."

I digested that and repeated myself, "We're safe in this storm? There seems to be a lot of lightning coming down."

"Yes, yes," she said. "Perfectly safe. That being said, it's probably best to set you on the next leg of your quest, Siegfried, and wrap things up here as quickly as possible."

"Again, I'm not Siegfried," I corrected her. "I'm not a hero. I'm not even a man. I'm self-evidently not who you seem to think I am." I offered my hand and introduced myself, while she ignored my introduction and studied me in confusion.

Continuing, I said, "I need your guidance. I've sworn an oath to establish my own merchant house that rivals those of my father and brother. I've pledged not to use resources from my family until I accomplish this on my own merits." She continued to look at me, increasingly bewildered. "I swore to the goddess Styx. I'm here seeking the mystic Sohvi for advice on how to do this. You are Sohvi, right?"

"Yes, of course I'm Sohvi. So, you ARE a hero, if you swore an oath and undertook a quest," she said, talking to me as if I was particularly dimwitted. "I think you're actually Siegfried too."

"Maybe this is a bad idea," I said. "Sorry for bothering you!" I began to walk away and a bold of lightning hit the ground fifteen feet ahead of me. An ozone smell hit me after the sound of thunder rolled over me. Turning back to the warrior woman, I said, "Or maybe we could talk a bit longer."

"You must defeat the evil vampire lurking in the farmhouse yonder," she pointed to a nearby home. "Wait for darkness, it will meet you in this field, and you will have a legendary battle that will last all night. With the last of your strength, you will deflect his final blow, then the first rays of the morning sun will destroy him and you will be triumphant."

"I'm completely ill-equipped to fight a vampire," I said. "I don't have a weapon, or any ability to fight. Whatsoever. I couldn't fight any monster for longer than a few seconds. If a vampire comes out of that farmhouse after dark I'm in big trouble and it's likely going to kill me in short order."

"Your bravery has fled, sweet Siegfried. I weep for you," she said, looking more irritated than weepy. "It isn't ideal, but you can go and slay the vampire before the sun sets. It will be sleeping in the cellar of the longhouse, so it's a coward's attack. Very womanly. But perhaps you'll recover your courage through a craven's triumph."

"We're both women, so I'm not sure why you're using womanly as a slur. I'm not even equipped to kill a sleeping vampire. I think I'd rather just leave," I said.

"Slay the vampire while it sleeps, or be hunted and killed after dark when he arises, I care not what you choose," she pronounced. She walked over to Pegasus and began climbing onto his back. The winged stallion cringed under the weight.

"There has to be a third option here," I shouted to her, following her to her mount. Pegasus nuzzled me and I pet his snout. "Maybe I could go with you?"

"Complete your quest, and I will take you to Odin the all-father. His wisdom and power will lay waste to all obstacles in your path and bring your journey to its end. But first, survive the vampire," she said. Smacking Pegasus, the winged stallion started running as best he could, taking flight and slowly gaining altitude. Bolts of lightning continued to shoot past them, interrupting their flight as they circled around me and departed back toward the east.

The storm left with them and in their wake I was left with a pleasant day for hiking, looking across at the farmhouse in the afternoon light.

WALKING AROUND THE FARMHOUSE, I found it was a neat, modern, well maintained structure. Tasteful curtains hung in the window, and inside it was decorated in nordic fashion, looking like an Ikea showroom to me. I was rounding the house to the front, when the door opened and a woman with an apron on looked out at me. She said something in Finnish then, seeing my blank look, said in English, "Are you ok? You seem lost."

Looking at the woman, I decided I didn't have any choice but to trust her. I said, "Ma'am, I'm in trouble."

"Ma'am?" she said, amused. "I'm only 30! It can't be as bad as all that."

"A valkyrie arrived with the storm you likely saw outside your window. She said a vampire lives in this house and after dark it's going to come out and kill me. She told me my only chance is to kill it in your cellar before it wakes up. Please help me, I don't know how to fight a vampire," I pleaded.

Looking me over, she burst into laughter. Seeing my serious expression she brought herself under control. "Someone is playing games with you," she said. "There's no

vampire living here. We don't even have a cellar! And I didn't
see or hear any storm. This isn't a large house. I can give you
a tour and convince you that there aren't any vampires here.
You can have dinner with my husband and me when he gets
home."

"Or," she continued. "We can take my car and drive you
back into town if you're afraid of the house. Whatever you'd
prefer."

Looking at her carefully, I said, "Let's do the tour if you
really don't mind. Is your husband a farmer?"

"No," she said. "He's a senior software engineer with
Google."

"So," said her husband Linus, "Should we eat here or go out
to a restaurant in case the vampire comes knocking?"

"Don't tease her," said the wife who had introduced
herself as Sari. "We should eat the pork and there's enough
for three."

"As long as we don't invite him in, I think we're ok," said
Linus. "I'm going to put a clove of garlic over the door and
each window. It can't hurt right? Where's the tape?" The
engineer began happily puttering as he put the garlic up
around the house.

"We should have a sauna after dinner," suggested Sari.
"What are you watching on Netflix?"

"I haven't been watching much TV recently," I admitted,
"but I was watching 'House of the Dragon' with a friend in
Toronto a few weeks back."

Sari said, "Ahh, 'House of the Dragon'! We haven't seen
that yet. We don't have HBO. We went to some of the places

they filmed 'Game of Thrones' when we visited Iceland a few years ago."

Sipping coffee, Linus looked proudly at the door. "After dark and no vampires. My garlic did the trick. So, tell us how you ended up meeting a valkyrie," he asked, and I told the story, starting at my birthday party.

Finishing with what led me to their farmhouse, Linus suddenly said, "I wonder if she meant the ghost next door?" Sari laughed.

"What ghost?" I asked.

"Legend has it that back in the 1920's there was a grizzly murder next door and a family of four were all slaughtered in their house," he began.

"Wasn't it a recently married couple?" asked Sari.

"Maybe," he admitted. "Or a bunch of kids who'd been left home alone. Someone died, anyways. Every owner of the house since has been run off. Every few years, someone buys the land and tries to build on it. The original house is just a ruin now, but before they begin construction, they always lose their nerve, sit on the property for a few years, then sell it to the next person."

"It's been nice for us, quiet neighbors," said Sari.

"Yes," said Linus. "I've walked around the land there and looked in the ruins of the house, but I've never seen anything unusual. Maybe you'll have better luck than I did," he gave a force, spooky laugh, "or worse luck!"

"Let's have that sauna. Us girls first, then you will have your turn Linus," decided Sari.

WALKING around the ruins of the old farmhouse, I wore the hardhat I'd borrowed from Linus and the hammer and measuring tape I'd borrowed from Sari. Sticking my head through the area that had once been a door, I loudly announced, "Yes, this will do quite nicely for the foundation." I measured the rotted timber at the bottom to see the width of the doorway. "Ah, yes. Thirty-six inches. That's very good." I took out the hammer and lightly tapped the three inches of door frame which was all that remained on the right hand side. It crumbled under the tap.

Walking around the perimeter, I continued, "A nice little attached garage is just the thing. No one likes going outside to get to their car. I wonder what sort of driveway I should make..."

As I turned to look in a window, an eldritch, glowing blue figure floated through the far rubble that had been a wall at one point. Our eyes met, and in a rush it flew across the room and abruptly stopped two inches from my face. It's phantom jaw unhinged and spread to an unnatural size as an unworldly scream of torment issued forth.

6

B linking twice at the horrifying spectacle, I screamed and stared at it, frozen in place.

The ghost and I looked at each other for several long seconds. It gave a second, less enthusiastic, unnatural scream.

"That's very frightening," I said, rooted where I stood. "I imagine most people are running in fear when they hear that." It kept it's eyes locked on mine and floated around me.

"Terrifying," I continued. "By any chance, does a vampire live here with you?"

"A vampire?" it asked. "Isn't a ghost scary enough?"

"Absolutely," I agreed.

"So why aren't you running away?" it asked. I began the story of my encounter with the valkyrie. The ghost got fed up half ways through and said, "I don't know what this has to do with me. There's no vampire here. I think you're at the wrong place." It's form had begun to distort and rather than looking like a fearsome banshee, he began to look like a glowing, blue, insubstantial teenage boy.

"Well, this Sohvi seemed confused. She kept insisting

that I'm Siegfried. There wasn't even a cellar in the house she directed me to. I'm thinking maybe she mistook you for a vampire," I explained.

"A ghost is nothing like a vampire!" he said.

"Well, sure. But a ghost is more like a vampire than a software engineer is, you'd have to admit that," I argued.

"What's a software engineer?" he asked.

"It's a computer thing," I explained.

"What's a computer?" he asked.

"It's a technology thing," I explained.

"Ohh, like cars?" he asked.

"Kind of," I said.

"Or, like electric lights?" he suggested.

"More like electric lights," I agreed. "How did you learn how to speak English?"

"I don't know English," he said. "How did you learn Finnish?"

"I don't know Finnish," I admitted. "It must be telepathy."

"What's telepathy?" he asked.

"It's when two peoples' minds connect directly and they send thoughts to one another," I explained.

"How are you going to slay me?" he asked.

"Honestly, I'm not sure I was going to slay the vampire. I'm certainly not going to slay you. I wouldn't know how to, either," I said.

"So, he says his name is Kauno, and his brother apparently killed him in the 1920's when he was thirteen," I explained to Linus and Sari. "They were wrestling, in the cellar, for whatever that's worth, and his brother hit him with a piece of stone and kept smashing his head until he was dead. It was apparently quite the scandal at the time. The brother went to juvenile detention, but the parents kept trying to help the older brother."

"He's angry that his parents didn't cast his brother out for killing him, that they kept trying to take care of his murderer. That's why he's still haunting the site and can't rest. I'm going to go into town tomorrow and do some research on the family."

"Can we go meet him?" Linus asked excitedly.

"No," said Sari. "We're not Americans who chase ghosts. We avoid them. We're not meeting him."

"Maybe he could come live with us if he's lonely?" suggested Linus. "We could play boardgames with him."

"Definitely not," decided Sari.

"Yes, I looked it up and apparently your brother got into legal trouble after a number of fairly serious assaults. He had multiple prison sentences and died, while incarcerated, when he was fifty-three," I said, referring to my notes.

Kauno looked at me impassively.

"Your parents kept trying to help him. Your father passed away a few years before your brother and your mother lived for around a decade after him," I finished. "Does knowing all that help at all?"

"I don't know," the ghost said. "What's supposed to happen if it helps?"

"I actually looked into that, too," I said. "It would have been easier to contact some of my family's experts and get the run down from them, but I was able to get a pretty good sense digging around on my own."

"The basic idea is that when most people pass away, their spirit merges with something important to them. This could be their house or a favorite possession. Often it can be into the general vicinity of where they lived or died, a forest, garden, or a battlefield. Rarely, they'll merge with another person, but the only real effect from that is that both spirits then pass into something else together after the surviving person dies. This happens sometimes with parents who are deeply committed to their children, or romantic soulmates."

"So, I'd probably merge with the countryside here, since i don't have children or a soulmate?" he asked.

"I guess," I said. "I'm really not an expert on this. I just tried to quickly get a general understanding."

"Maybe if you were my soulmate, I could merge with you," he suggested.

"Maybe," I responded doubtfully. "I don't think either of us really feels like soulmates."

"No," he agreed. "I'm just so angry at everything that my brother took from me. My life, career, romances... everything."

"Yeah, I get that," I said. "But I don't see what you can do about that now that he's gone. Scaring off people who want to live on the site of your old house doesn't seem to be making you happy."

"I hate being alone, then hate having company," he said. "Even you get on my nerves sometimes. No offense."

"None taken," I said. "We'll sort this out one way or another."

I WAS WALKING BACK from the ghost's ruin to Linus and Sari's place when a storm started brewing in the east again.

Watching Sohvi's approach, I saw that she was no longer riding Pegasus, but instead was on some sort of reptilian flying creature. Lightning struck the charred tree stumps as she approached.

On their final approach, I saw how unsteadily the new mount seemed to be flying. Getting nervous at how directly they were coming at me, I ran out of the way and turned in time to see it land, traveling too quickly, on the creature's hind legs. It's front legs and claws seemed to be merged with its wings. As its rear claws caught, the momentum slammed the creature into the ground and threw Sohvi over its head, through the air, and to the ground. Again she left a trough in the sod.

I approached her as she adjusted her armor and retrieved her spear and helmet.

"What happened to Pegasus?" I asked.

"He's incompetent," she said curtly. "I had to requisition a new mount."

I asked, "What's this one's name?"

She replied, "No name yet."

"How about Siegfried," I suggested.

"You want me to name my wyvern after you?" she asked, perplexed.

Shaking my head, I repeated, "I'm not Siegfried. I don't know why you think I am. By the way, I went looking for that vampire you sent me after and it doesn't exist."

"You didn't kill the vampire?" she asked, angrily. "I assumed since you were still alive you'd have done your duty. What's the problem? Do 'vampire lives matter', snowflake?"

"What?" I asked. "What, WHAT, *WHAT*? How are you riffing on 'lives matter' when you don't even realize that Siegfried has been dead for hundreds of years?"

We glared at one another for a few moments.

I continued, "The farmhouse you directed me to not only didn't have a vampire in it, it didn't possess a cellar, which is where you claimed the vampire would be found. I investigated the local area and found a ghost at the ruins of a neighbors house."

"Can't even find a vampire, let alone slay one, and now you're trying to substitute slaying something easier like a ghost?" Sohvi asked.

"I didn't slay him," I answered. "I'm trying to help him. Lead him to the light or finding peace or whatever."

"You didn't even slay the ghost!?!" she said, indignantly.

"I have no idea what you want me to do," I explained slowly. "You're giving me terrible instructions and bad information."

"Fine," she said, giving me a dirty look. "Let's keep your next task simple. Gather stinging nettle, dandelion, juniper, heather, goutweed, and birch. You must gather them yourself, under moonlight of course, and you can't buy them in a shop or hire someone to collect them. Brew them into a tea and drink it. This will purify you and prepare you for the next task."

"Fine," I said, eyeing the valkyrie suspiciously.

"Fine," she responded, and began mounting her wyvern to leave.

7

"Well, that's everything except the birch," I said to Linus and Sari. "That's lucky that you had dandelion and goutweed in your yard. Definitely gave me a head start."

"You can get birch about 20 minutes walk that way," Linus pointed to a stand of trees that could be clearly seen in the light of the full moon. "Let's go!"

"It's getting late," observed Sari. "Could we get the birch tomorrow?"

I said, "I'm not sure if I'm supposed to collect it all in one night. I think I'll go grab it, just to be sure. You two head home, I'll be back in half an hour or so."

"No, you shouldn't wander alone. I'll come with you," said Linus.

"She told you to go home," said Sari. "We'll stay up waiting for you. Call if you run into any trouble."

Swinging my basket, I walked towards the stand of trees. I started thinking about Sohvi's vampire and wondered if maybe I should have left this for another night.

Reaching the trees, I found some branches with small, newly opened leaves and collected them. I also cut a few branches for the sauna. I was just packing up my things to leave, when I heard a heavy, throaty panting behind me.

Turning slowly, I saw a seven foot tall, humanoid beast standing on two legs. Shredded pants clung to its legs, and a belt remained about it's waist. Bits of fabric remained wrapped around his arms and tatters of a shirt hung from its chest. Brown fur covered all its visible body and a long snout broke into a loud howl as it raised its canine head into the night air. Fearsome teeth lined its jaw.

Eyeing me menacingly, it moved its face closer to mine. Drool ran down its chin and sprayed me when it exhaled.

"Ok, I love everything about this," I said looking him in the eye. "But we have to go over a few ground rules first."

Coming up short, the beast stared at me. "What?" he said, his speech slurred by the bestial tongue in his long mouth.

"I had a werewolf boyfriend, back in college," I said. "I read a lot of dark romance and I'm totally team Jacob."

"Bah, Twilight," the beast sneered.

"I don't want to contract lycanthropy, curing it is a real pain. So no breaking the skin. Light scratches are fine, but be careful with your teeth and claws," I explained. "It's fine if you rip any of these clothes, although that'll be a bit of an awkward situation to explain when I get back to Linus and Sari. Except this bra. It's my favorite. Do you want me to take it off first or can you be careful with it? And, incidentally, do we need to worry about a vampire while we're out here?" I began reaching out towards the monster's snout, then pulled my hand back as he snapped at me.

"You don't understand, you stupid cunt," he said. "I'm going to kill you here and eat your warm liver. I don't usually play with my food, but I'm going to make your last minutes of life excruciating."

"Well, I don't love the C-word, but if that works for you I can deal with it. What's your plan for dealing with regent Ellisar of the High Park elven court?" I asked. "You do realize I'm under their protection, right?"

"What?" he asked awkwardly again.

"Ellisar, the regent of the Toronto elven court," I explained. "They're my friend. At the tribunal a couple months ago I 'cracked them up'. They told me how they miss fox hunts from back in the day, but hunts are just so out of fashion now. If you infect me with lycanthropy, injure me, and certainly if you kill me, you're going to have an elven host coming to Finland on vacation to hunt you down and skin you alive."

"Also," I continued, "I'm the wayward daughter and heir of, arguably, the preeminent merchant house. My brother's house is regarded as number one, so I suppose I'm the heir to the number 2 house. My parents and brother would be racing the elves to deliver their justice to you. I can show you emails on my phone with all these people if you have any doubts."

"We can still have some fun," I continued. "Just stay in my boundaries. No penetration, but boob stuff is fine. What do we think about the bra? Why don't I just take it off to be on the safe side?"

Vibrating in frustration, the beast rocked from side-to-side. Howling again, he snapped in my direction then began loping away from me, disappearing into the night.

∾

LAYING BACK IN THE SAUNA, I finished telling Sari my werewolf story. We had shared the leftover 'purification' tea that I had made and drank some of the night before.

"That was a bold gambit! What would you have done if he'd wanted to fool around with you?" Sari asked. We had gotten in the sauna after Linus left for work and were building up a good sweat. I wore a towel and Sari was relaxing Finnish style.

"Heh, then we would have fooled around I guess," I admitted with a nervous chuckle.

"Do you really like werewolves that much," she asked.

I responded, "I do. It's a shame things never worked out with Mark. He was my werewolf boyfriend in college. He's becoming a buddhist monk in Thailand now."

"Why did you let him run away to Thailand?" she asked.

"The sex was great, but everything else was just ok," I explained. "The only, minor, issue with the sex was I'd always end up with hairs in my mouth. One time, he actually wanted me to 'acknowledge my rich, female, privilege' if you can believe that. He always had a chip on his shoulder about my family's money, but his mother was a dentist in the Bay Area. I always felt like he was throwing stones in a glass house, you know?"

"Hmm," she acknowledged my story. "Flog me with the birch whip you brought back."

"Flog you?" I asked with a chuckle.

"Is that not the right word?" she clarified. "You strike with the branch and it helps the circulation. We call it a vihta."

"I guess so," I said. "Flog usually means a real punishment. Maybe whip or whisk would be the right term. Even whip is a bit violent."

"Whisk me with the vihta then," she clarified.

I READ over the emails from my family. With my advice my father had smoothed things over with Drigrin. They also took my advice and had Sheena take the finance bros out to a strip club. She'd embarrassed them enough that they hadn't brought it up again since. My mother wrote about how Mrs. Silverberg kept hounding her about me going to work for her.

I'd emailed the elven court and told them my experience with the werewolf. I left out the sexy time part, but I told them how I'd threatened him and gotten him to back down. I didn't think he'd retaliate, but it'd help them track him down if anything else happened. The regent wrote back and said they wanted to organize a hunt, just to punish him for his impertinence. I wrote back and told them that probably wasn't a good idea. An email from Vaeril said they were coming to protect me, which had been sent nine hours ago and said they'd be leaving immediately, so it was probably too late to stop them. I sent off a reply trying, just in case.

"So, did this valkyrie tell you how to slay me?" the ghost Kauno asked me. "I'm not sure whether or not I want to be slain. Maybe it would be better than this tormented existence..."

"I'm not going to slay you," I said emphatically. "I don't know how and didn't ask. I've brewed and drank the tea, so we'll see what happens next with Sohvi."

"I've been thinking about it and I don't think I could merge with anything permanently, but I think I could attach myself to you. If it was useful for us to go somewhere else together. Maybe I could scare the valkyrie for you," the ghost suggested.

"I don't think she's smart enough to get scared," I said.

Vaeril and Sohvi glared at one another. Lightning bolts periodically crashed into the ground around us. The valkyrie's latest mount, a giant eagle, was recovering from their crash landing.

"What happened to Siegfried?" I asked.

"He died centuries ago and is now in Valhalla," Sohvi said. "Why do you ask?"

"No, Siegfried your wyvern mount," I clarified.

"Ahh," she said. "He was no good. So, did you run into the wolfie while you were gathering herbs?"

"You knew about the werewolf?" I asked, shocked.

"Of course," she said, smugly. "The whole point of sending you out was to get you to slay him."

I related my experience with the werewolf. As elf and valkyrie listened to my story, Vaeril looked increasingly scandalized and Sohvi looked increasingly angry.

"So, instead of killing the werewolf, you tried to jump him?" she asked. "This isn't any way for a hero to behave." She gave us both a dirty look before continuing. "This is really your last chance, if you mess this up again I don't know what I'm going to do with you." She handed me a map. "Here are directions to a cave that's infested with giant rats. Go and kill them, then I'll take you to visit Frigga."

"You were going to take me to see Odin," I said.

"Yes, to visit Odin," she said.

I continued, "I keep telling you, I'm not a hero, I can't kill giant rats."

"I shall slay the rats on your behalf," promised Vaeril.

"So there you go. Have your henchman kill them, spread out some poison, or build a better rat trap," she advised.

"Ok, I'll do that," I agreed. The elf and the valkyrie resumed glaring at one another.

8

Moving along the rough-hewn passageway, Vaeril lifted their torch higher and we peered into the gloom.

"Are you sure we wouldn't be better off with a flashlight or something?" I asked. "I haven't seen any giant rats yet."

They replied, "This is a good, proper elven torch. Can't be beat. Do you smell that?"

"Yes," I said thoughtfully, coming to a stop. "A sulfur smell. Are there hot springs in this area?"

"No, not in this area," said the elf thoughtfully. "It could be from demonic teleportation, but the cloud of brimstone that accompanies that usually dissipates pretty quickly."

"They add a sulphuric smell to natural gas and propane for home usage," I suggested. "Can't imagine how that would be in this cave though."

"Some sewers get a sulfur smell to them," they said. "This doesn't smell like that and I can't imagine it would be that strong. The ancient Egyptians and Greeks did some industrial work that had a sulphuric smell to them. For bleaching cotton, religious ceremonies, and fumigating."

"I think some accounts of alien abductions and encounters have mentioned sulfur," I said, thinking back to a book I read as a girl.

The elf asked, "What's an alien?"

"A being from another planet; they come from outer space to visit Earth," I explained.

"Are they real?" they asked, curiously.

I said, "I don't think so. So we can probably rule aliens out."

"Of course, a smell of sulfur could be the most obvious thing," the elf said, with a nervous chuckle.

"What's the most obvious thing," I asked.

They held the elven torch up and looked ahead apprehensively. "It's impossible, no reason to think that. Perhaps we should think about leaving..."

Turning around, I saw that a rough, stone wall had appeared about a foot behind us and now blocked our escape. "Uh, Vaeril?" The elf looked at the newly appeared wall, squeaked, then began feeling along it, searching for any secrets.

"What smells like sulfur?" I asked.

"Demons teleporting, hot springs, aliens, sewage," the elf began reciting as they searched more frantically.

"What else?" I asked flatly.

"Natural gas and propane in human houses, ancient human industrial application," they continued. "And... dragons."

Deeper in the cave, a low, throaty chuckling noise could be heard.

"I don't think there's any way except forward, do you?" I asked the elf. Finishing their investigation of the newly arrived wall, they nodded sadly. We resumed our movement into the mountain. Reaching the end of the corridor, the passage opened up into a massive, dark cavern. The smell of sulfur had become overwhelming and Vaeril and I sweated profusely.

"It's gotten rather warm, hasn't it?" asked the elf. I realized they were right.

A burst of fire lit up the cavern and spread out in a complicated pattern. The flames illuminated a massive, reptilian form, lying prone on the far side of the cavern. A number of torches were ignited by the flames. A wave of heat slammed into the elf and me.

"We aren't thieves!" I proclaimed. "We ended up here accidentally. Please let us leave!"

The low chuckling sounded again. "Let me assure you, there's nothing accidental about your arrival," the drake said, its voice loud and clear. The reptilian god's lips moved as it talked. "And what would you be after if you were thieves?"

"Thieves, which we are not, might be after your treasure. Gold, and whatnot. We can pay you to let us go," I offered.

"Talk less," Vaeril whispered. "We're in trouble."

"Don't follow your elf friend's advice," suggested the dragon. "I've enjoyed your talking so far."

"We only wished to have a look at you and see if you were truly as great as tales say," I said. "I did not believe them."

"I know that you weren't expecting to find a dragon, so your words are clearly false," said the creature. "You're quoting something, but I'm not familiar with the source."

"It's from J.R.R. Tolkein's book 'The Hobbit'," I admitted. "The main character, Bilbo Baggins, flatters the dragon Smaug."

"Smaug? There aren't any dragons named Smaug. That's

a good name though," said the dragon. "Flatter me, or do not. It doesn't matter to me either way. Call me whatever you want, 'dragon' would work just fine. I was called Zosime a long time ago if you prefer that."

"Zosime, that's a human name isn't it?" I asked.

"Yes," said Zosime. "Greek, and given to me by a friend a long time ago."

"You said it isn't an accident that we're here," I asked. "We were looking to kill some giant rats. If you have a rat problem, we can deal with it for you."

"Manipulating the incompetent valkyrie was trivial," he said. "There aren't any rats here."

"My friend is frightened," I said. "Would you please let them leave?"

"Not yet," said the dragon. "They will be useful in our conversation. They aren't in any immediate danger. I know all about you, my princess. Your ritual, your family, and your activities. Perhaps you could introduce me to your friend."

"This is Vaeril, but I'm not a princess," I objected.

"Vaeril," the dragon said, tasting the name. "Which of the Canadian courts are you from?"

"High Park, lord dragon," said Vaeril. "How do you know where I'm from if you didn't know my name?"

"Your accent, first and most obviously," began Zosime. "There's linguist drift, but it's unmistakably Canadian. Your clothes were clearly made by the elven tailor Myrin. They've adjusted how they stitch the inseam. I like it. Myrin belonged to the High Park court 100 years ago and I suppose is still there. Yes, given our friend's expression they're still there. There's the small possibility of movement between the courts or the formation of new courts, but your reaction clearly tells me that hasn't happened. There was a small possibility of the Stanley Park court splintering, and a much smaller chance of High Park splintering."

Vaeril's mouth hung open as they looked at the dragon.

"Not a princess?" said Zosime continuing, "Are you not from a wealthy family?"

"I am, but...," I began.

"Are you not well educated?" he continued.

"Yes, but...," I tried again.

"Haven't you been well nourished and medically cared for?" he asked.

"Now there's more...," I responded.

"Yes, of course, you have. And your objection is that your parents weren't monarchs. The bloodline never mattered to me. Princesses just made good companions," the drake finished. "And you are a princess."

"Why would you want a companion?" I asked.

"Tell me your best guess why I'd want a companion?" he asked. His head moved forward on a long, serpentine neck, drawing closer to us.

"Given all the information you seem to be picking up from us, I'd guess that you get a companion in order to learn about the world. Pick up information about what's changed outside since your last companion," I said.

Looking at me steadily, the dragon responded, "You're a clever one. None of the others guessed correctly the first time. I think I'm going to enjoy the next few decades. From the smell of you, you're in good health. Any medical interventions shouldn't be needed for a long time yet."

"While I'm happy to help you access news, I can't stay here," I objected. "And please don't sniff me, it's creepy."

"You can and you will," said Zosime.

"There must be some alternative," I objected. "Some

bargain we can make. What do you want? What could we exchange for my freedom?"

"You are what I want. You have nothing else I want and I could get anything else far more easily than you could provide it," said the dragon. "Traditionally, a champion is allowed to battle me to the death for your freedom." His eyes glanced at the elf. "The elf has no chance against me, and their death would be an unfortunate way for us to begin our friendship. Your grief would color our interactions for the next three years or so. I will give you that option, however."

Vaeril swallowed repeatedly and looked up at the dragon's bulk. "I... will be her champion," they stammered.

"No!" I said. "I don't accept you as my champion. Zosime, will I be allowed to come and go from this cave?"

"We will both remain here for every moment of the remainder of your life," he answered.

Looking up at the huge creature thoughtfully, I was about to speak when he cut me off. "I know what you're thinking and it won't work."

"What am I thinking?" I asked.

"You're about to threaten me with retaliation," he said. "First from your elf friend's court, then from your family, then perhaps from the other merchant families, or the Norse pantheon. If you feel desperate enough you might even imply you have a dangerous ghost who will come after you, a couple of werewolf boyfriends, or a friend from Ukraine and you'll try to convince me he had some sort of special forces training before he became a bellboy. After all that fails to impress me, you'll try to invent some more threatening friends."

I asked, "Rasmus is from Ukraine?"

"He is," the dragon said. "None of your friends are the slightest threat to me. They would be wise to avoid me entirely, but if they came looking for us they'd never find us. If I ever allowed them to find us, it would go badly for them."

"Is this some sort of sex thing?" I asked, suddenly suspicious.

The dragon's head pulled back. "Sex thing? Why do you princesses always think it's a sex thing? It's like asking someone if they have sex with their dog! No, it isn't a sex thing. That's disgusting and offensive."

"Do you transform into other shapes, like a human form?" I asked.

"I could, I suppose, but I can't imagine why I would," he said.

"Why not? Wouldn't it be useful to be in human form? You could go and gather information about the world?" I suggested.

"Have you ever sought out someone to transform you into a cockroach so you could scurry through cracks and eat garbage?" the dragon asked.

"No," I admitted.

"Well, there you go, I'm not interested in that either," he said. "As a sign of my benevolence and to start things off on the right foot, I'm willing to allow Vaeril to leave. They're to never mention anything they've experienced in my lair. If they do, I'll know and it won't go well for them or their court."

"I'm not going anywhere," said Vaeril.

"So bold," observed the dragon. "You're welcome to stay as long as you want, of course. But once you leave you're forbidden to return. Princess, shall we wager on how long until they go? I'm willing to take over or under six months."

"Your cruelty seems quite calculated," I observed. "The only time you show any nastiness is when you're encouraging me to do what you want. There doesn't seem to be any way for me to escape my enslavement."

"Clever girl," observed the dragon.

"You're quite clear about me being your prisoner, not Vaeril. So there's something about me specifically you want, an elf won't give you the information you're looking for," I continued.

"Perhaps this princess is too clever," he said flatly.

"Why always princesses?" I asked. "Why don't you ever abduct a prince?"

He replied, "You already know the answer to that."

I said, "Because princes are valuable and people would come looking for them. Princesses are disposable and, if it's too much trouble, you can get away with snatching one of them."

"From the sounds of it, this isn't the obvious truth it once was. Human views on gender are shifting. Perhaps I will try a prince for my next companion," he said. "I grow weary of your game, spring your trap and be done with it."

"I challenge you to fight to the death and I will serve as my own champion," I declared.

"What are you doing?" asked Vaeril, horrified. "This is suicide!"

Pulling back into the darkness, Zosime angrily said, "The way out is clear, be gone before I change my mind and make a meal out of both of you."

Vaeril looked confused.

"If he kills me, he loses what he wants, a companion for decades to come," I explained. Walking towards the dragon I continued. "He doesn't want to kill me pointlessly when it won't get him what he wants. None of the previous princesses were willing to put themselves on the line, I take it?"

"Of the eleven possible ways to escape my enslavement, I've always considered this the most obvious. You may be the first to think of it, but I'm not impressed. It just lowers my esteem of the capabilities of your predecessors. Taunt me further at your peril, I grow weary of your presence."

"It's strange that you view this as taunting," I said, drawing closer. "I think it's been a long time since you talked to someone who wasn't a prisoner, or afraid of you."

His head shot forward out of the darkness and stopped suddenly inches from my face. I flinched slightly. He breathed in deeply and I was pulled forward slightly with the air. The pupils on the sides of his head watched me steadily.

"Don't even think it," he said.

"I wasn't," I said with a laugh.

"What were you going to do?" asked Vaeril.

"Nothing," I said, chuckling.

"She was going to pet my snout," said the drake. "Too familiar," he admonished.

"So," I said, "what I propose is that I'll get some books and information that I think you'll find useful. I'll come and visit and bring you more and we can set you up with an internet connection and the ability to get information about the world that way. We can talk when I'm here, or even when I'm not if we can get you set up with a phone or email. Maybe WhatsApp."

"You'll swear to return on a set schedule for the rest of your life," he insisted.

"No," I said. "I'll come back, when I want to, as your FRIEND. If you treat me decently, I'll come back sooner. If you're a jerk, it'll take longer or I'll stop coming altogether."

"Locking you up seems simpler," suggested Zosime.

"You think you're funny, but you aren't," I said.

The dragon responded, "All my previous princesses told me I'm hilarious."

"Well, you haven't convinced me yet," I said.

9

Standing in the field, along with Vaeril, the valkyrie Sohvi recovered from her crash on a large, multicolored bird she had been riding. The ghost Kauno had attached himself to my forearm. The tingling and glow after he merged had vanished.

"What's this you're riding now," I asked politely, gesturing at the large bird.

"Giant budgie," Sohvi said absently. "How'd things go with the dragon?"

"The dragon that was supposed to be a bunch of giant rats," I said pointedly.

"All you had to do is survive, I can be more generous with dragons. Still, I'd be impressed if you slew the foul wyrm!" She looked at me hopefully.

"He tried to take me prisoner," I said.

Looking thoughtful, Sohvi said, "They usually only do that to princesses."

"Apparently I am a princess, according to his definition," I replied.

"Did you correct him and tell him you're a hero?" she

asked.

"Well," I said with exasperation, "as I keep telling you, I'm not a hero. So, no."

"Ah well, at least you survived. It'll just be you coming, the elf and the ghost will have to remain behind," the valkyrie said. She flicked her finger next to my forearm and Kauno shot out of my body and flew back ten feet or so. Once we were separated, he began to be drawn towards his ruined house. He reached for me and called something as he picked up speed and was sucked over the horizon.

Sohvi mounted the bird and patted the seat behind her. I looked skeptically at the ill fitted saddle. "Perhaps I could ride in front of you? I don't want to fall off."

"You want to ride in front of me? Like a child?" the valkyrie asked, with contempt.

"Sure," I agreed and climbed up in front of her. "Please keep ahold of me!"

Launching into the air, Vaeril watched from the ground as we departed eastward. "Onwards to meet Thor," called out Sohvi.

"Odin!" I cried out as a lightning bolt passed by us in a boom of thunder.

LANDING GRACEFULLY on a sun lit rolling meadow, Sohvi helped me off of the giant budgie's back. "Odin's longhouse, as promised." She gestured to the longhouse fifty feet away.

"You'll take me home after I've met with the all-father?" I verified.

"I'll be waiting right here, hero," she assured me.

Walking over to the longhouse, I knocked on the wooden door. "Enter, hero!" I heard from inside. Opening the door, I saw a long, empty corridor with torches blazing along its walls. A robust, nordic looking man sat on a wooden throne on a raised dais. Empty tables with benches lined the hall leading to the god at the end.

Walking along the hall, I approached and greeted the god. "Hail, Odin All-Father! I have endured many trials to meet with you and beg a boon," I said.

"Welcome to Breidablik. I'm sorry, my daughter, but you mistake me for my father," the muscular warrior said. "I am Baldur, but I will assist you in any way I can."

"Baldur," I said. Trying to remember my norse mythology, I asked, "You're the god of death and resurrection? I thought you were condemned to remain in Hel because of a giantess. Is that right?"

"Yes, Tokk," Baldur said, looking uncomfortable. "Technically, I am still in Hel. That's my permanent residence. I'm only visiting here."

"How long have you been visiting?" I asked.

"Oh, probably for eight hundred years or so now. But I live in Hel," he insisted. "Hela required many oaths and promises before she'd agree to this visit."

Launching into an explanation, I told the god about my adventures to date. He listened attentively, making sympathetic noises at the appropriate places. After I'd finished my tale, I asked him if he'd be able to help me.

"Well, I'll certainly do everything I can to assist you, brave hero!" he said encouragingly.

"Could you help me form a merchant house that rivals my father and brother's?" I asked.

"Alas, such a feat would be the purview of my brother Njörðr. Or maybe one of his children. Certainly one of the Vanir. I am sworn not to intrude on their domains of influence," he explained sadly.

I thought for a few minutes about another request.

"Could you give me your wisdom or guidance, even if you can't intercede on my behalf with your divine powers?" I asked.

"Alas, I am forbidden from doing even that," he explained. I paused, disappointed, then thought some more.

"Could you help my friend Kauno? He's a ghost who has been stuck haunting the ruins of his family's house for decades. I want to help him move on," I said.

"A noble endeavor!" Baldur said approvingly. "Alas, I've sworn to Hela not to take any action that will affect her realm. Changing the movement of ghosts and souls would violate this oath."

Thinking about Baldur's domain, I asked, "Could you resurrect him? Give him a chance to live his life again and hopefully have a better death?".

"If only I could," he said sorrowfully. "This would fall under the movement of souls and ghosts."

In desperation, I requested, "Could you help me get to Odin or someone else who might help me?"

"That would be my brother Meili's domain," Baldur explained. "I am foresworn from meddling in his sphere of influence."

"Given everything I've told you, is there anything you can do to help me in any way?" I asked, running out of hope.

"I can commend you on your noble adventures and upstanding conduct to date," he said enthusiastically. "You have all the encouragement I can possibly offer. I'm rooting for you!"

I gave the god a weak smile. "Well, thanks for that, I suppose."

"Please return anytime in the future I can be of further service," he said, beaming down at me from his dias.

I gave the god a nod and departed from his longhouse. Looking around the sunlit meadow, there was no sign of Sohvi or her giant budgie. I sighed.

WALKING THROUGH THE MEADOW AIMLESSLY, I checked my phone for the third time before remembering that there wasn't any cell service in Asgard. Small hills dotted the countryside. In the distance I saw a wall of some sort and walked towards it. It felt like I had been walking long enough for night to fall, but still the sun shone on the meadow I was walking through. A group of figures were gathered a short distance past the wall and, as I drew closer to them, half of them waved to me.

Getting closer, I saw that the stone wall was about three feet high and the group of men were an odd assortment. Many looked like viking warriors, with battle axes and horned helmets. Others had plate armor and looked like medieval knights. A small number were dressed in modern military uniforms from the last hundred years. In addition to these warriors, there were a few men and women in business suits and an eight year old boy in shorts and a T-shirt.

I climbed over the wall and approached this unusual group.

"Hail warrior, welcome to the fields of Valhalla and your eternal reward!" one of the vikings boomed. "We're eager to hear tales of your exploits and how you fell in battle."

"I'm not a warrior," I explained. "I haven't fallen in battle. A valkyrie brought me to meet Baldur and she left, so I'm trying to find my way home. On Earth. Ideally in Finland, but really anywhere on Earth would do. I can get around the planet ok on my own once I get back."

The group began whispering worriedly to one another. One of the viking warriors began greeting me the same way the first had and the spirits around him shushed him. Finally, one of the men in a business suit said, "That's all well and good, but perhaps you could still tell us about some of your exploits. We're waiting here to ambush another group of warriors and we've been waiting quite a while. All of us have told our stories and we'd love to hear yours!"

One of the viking warriors started to tell me the story of his death, but another warrior interrupted him and said, "We've all heard it before."

I launched in to the story of my adventures so far. When I got to the part with the werewolf, an excited murmur ran through the group.

"You should have hit him on the head with a silver mace," suggested one viking.

"I didn't have any weapons, let alone a mace, certainly not one made out of silver," I said.

"You should have shot him with a silver bullet," said one of the soldiers in a World War 2 Nazi uniform.

"I didn't have any weapons, let alone a gun, certainly not one with silver bullets," I said. "I've also never fired a gun before."

"Perhaps you could have used unarmed combat to turn his strength against him," suggested a samurai.

Shrugging, I said, "I dropped out of judo after one session. I don't know any unarmed combat."

"You should have invoked some sort of diplomatic protection, given him a reason why he wasn't allowed to attack you," suggested one of the men in a suit. The vikings sneered at this suggestion.

"That isn't real combat!" protested a viking.

"Then why am I here?" asked the lawyer. "I died during a legal battle and ended up in Valhalla. You might not like it, but the fact that I'm here proves that it counts."

The vikings muttered quietly at this, then conceded the point.

I continued with my explanation of the encounter with the werewolf, giving them all the details since I figured they wouldn't have anyone to gossip about me behind my back. Most of the warriors were scandalized, but the lawyers were impressed. "This is a new form of battle!" said one of the female lawyers. "She's a warrior!"

The eight year old expressed confusion and the rest of the warriors ignored him.

Continuing my story, the warriors listened as I described my encounter with the dragon. They again suggested attacks that were impossible for me to execute and wouldn't have worked if I could have.

"So, she won the battle by offering to die?" asked one of the vikings. "This doesn't make any sense. It's either genius or madness." The warriors all began excitedly debating it.

"How did you die?" I asked the eight year old.

"I was in the middle of a spelling bee, we went for lunch on the break, and I choked on my burger," he said sadly.

"How do you like living... er... being here?" I asked.

"We have lots of fun!" he said. "I miss my mom and dad of course, but every day we break into teams and have a big battle. Once a team wins, we all come back to life and eat all night. Then in the morning we do it all over again. It's like a paintball fight! These guys have been teaching me how to endure dying each time I'm killed and all sorts of ways to fight. The lawyers taught me how to file an amicus brief, but I haven't had a chance to do that yet."

"Wow, neat!" I said.

"We have decided," one of the vikings stepped forward as the spokesman of the group. "That you are, indeed, a great warrior. Possibly a hero!"

"I'm not a hero," I objected.

"A hero, I say!" he said. "And as such we will offer to come to you in your hour of greatest need to help you. In exchange, should you fall in battle and come to Valhalla after your death, you will join our team in the daily battles!"

"I hope that doesn't happen, but ok. That's great, thanks!" I said, looking at the smiling faces. A Nazi's toothy grin made me uncomfortable. "But, before that happens, could you help me get back to Earth?"

"It will take great strategic cunning, and place us at a disadvantage in today's battle, but we will lead you to Heimdall, guardian of the Bifrost bridge. He will get you home."

"Heimdall, like in the Marvel movies?" I asked. "Perfect!"

Moving cautiously, the group of warriors guided me across the battlefield.

WE WERE WALKING along a path and the eight year old asked me if I had a dictionary. He was disappointed when I admitted that I didn't. Nevertheless, he was quietly practicing spelling with me when a man came running out of a nearby woods, charging at our group with something in his hand.

Responding with military precision, a number of bullets hit the attacker, followed by a number of arrows. He stumbled, fell to the ground, then erupted in a giant ball of flame, engulfing part of our group.

Pain exploded around me as I was consumed by fire and every part of my body hurt. And then everything went black.

10

Returning to consciousness on a massive field, I rose and saw that I was surrounded by countless people. Most were also picking themselves up off of the ground. Trumpets were sounding and a group of people in ninja garb stood silently on a raised platform. Some of those gathered gave half-hearted applause, while others booed them.

Slipping off the platform, the ninjas entered an enormous longhouse and everyone assembled started moving to follow them. Two viking warriors approached me, clapped me on the back, and greeted me. I assumed they must have been part of the group I'd been in.

They told me one of them had been injured in the blast and died after limping along for a couple hours afterwards and the other had been run down by a knight's charge. As we got closer to the entrance, more members of our group joined us and most of them were with us by the time we headed to the tables they usually sat at.

"Remember where we are and you can join us at night," one of the lawyers told me.

"I'm hoping I won't be here on any future night," I responded. "Why are there so many lawyers here?"

"Apparently every legal case is a battle," she explained. "Any lawyer who dies with an open case ends up here. I suppose the retired lawyers go somewhere else, but most practicing lawyers will always have a number of cases open at once."

A viking next to me filled my glass with mead and slapped me on the back as I took a tentative sip. As I was choking, he asked me how I liked dying in an explosion.

"It hurt," I said.

"Ha, ha," he said, amused. "There's a trick to that. Firstly, you want to separate the sensation from any value judgement. Don't think about how much you hate the person who hurt you or how you'll get revenge. Don't complain, even to yourself, about how unfair it is that it happened to you. Focus on the sensation you're feeling instead. Dying fast in an explosion like that, it's one of the better ways to die."

A Roman centurion cut in, giving the viking a dirty look. "Second, consider the consequence of good versus bad coping. Will rolling around on the ground moaning help you feel better? Will screaming your throat raw improve your situation? Think about you as an individual, detached from your body, and how the real you isn't harmed. Right now, are you in any pain?"

I shook my head.

A man dressed like a cowboy cut in next. "Third, how awful is the pain? As we die repeatedly here, we find most deaths aren't as bad as the worst we've experienced. Most of us would be delighted to die quickly like you did, as the second best outcome to victory."

The eight year old cut in and said, "Finally, think about your ability to cope. Compare your current situation to what you've survived in the past. Think about this as exercising your coping skills and demonstrating what you can endure. All these techniques amount to the same thing. Accept what's happening to you and it will bother you less than if you fight it or rail against it."

I was digesting this when a familiar looking man approached the table and flashed finger guns at us. The table booed him and some people threw food at him. Finally, I recognized him as the attacker who had killed me. A samurai got up and gave him a hearty handshake in greeting. The viking next to me said, "They have a mutual friend who was a kamikaze pilot."

I nibbled at some roast boar. I didn't feel hungry or full, no matter how much I consumed. Over the course of the night, we ate steadily. Some of the deceased warriors insisted I learn combat skills from them and they took turns tutoring me.

Hours later, a voice called, "Dawn!' and everyone started walking towards the doors.

"What happens if we stay here and don't go outside?" I asked one of the vikings near me.

"You'd miss all the fun," he said, putting his arm around me, and roughly pulling me towards the exit.

As I walked through the doorway, I immediately found myself behind a desk in a courtroom. The judge sat behind his desk and on the other side of the room I saw a Native American man decked out for war, standing behind a desk with a client sitting next to him. He made eye contact with me, then flashed a rude gesture towards me beneath his desk.

"The court - the court will come to order. The Rev. Cartwright will open court with a prayer."

I looked around, trying to figure out what was happening. As the prayer concluded, the judge called the case. "State of Tennessee vs John Thomas Scopes."

THE JUDGE SAID, "Mr. Scopes, the jury has found you guilty under this indictment, charging you with having taught in the schools of Rhea county, in violation of what is commonly known as the anti-evolution statute, which makes it unlawful for any teacher to teach in any of the public schools of the state, supported in whole or in part by the public school funds of the state, any theory that denies the story of the divine creation of man, and teach instead thereof that man has descended from a lower order of animals."

"The jury have found you guilty. The statute makes this an offense punishable by a fine of not less than $100 nor more than $500. The court now finds itself in the unfortunate position, due to numerous errors committed by the incompetent prosecution, of having to overturn this verdict and enter an unjust ruling of not guilty."

"Oh-Have you anything to say, Mr. Scopes?"

The defendant J. T. Scopes said, "Your honor, while I'm happy I have been found not guilty, I feel that I have been charged of violating an unjust statute. I will continue in the future, as I have in the past, to oppose this law in any way I can. Any other action would be in violation of my ideal of academic freedom - that is, to teach the truth as guaranteed in our constitution of personal and religious freedom. I think the law is unjust."

As agony shot through my body, I looked down to see myself disintegrating and falling apart into black dust.

I FOUND myself on the ground where I woke up the night before. Rising, I saw one of the lawyers from our group standing on the platform. She raised her briefcase in the air as trumpets sounded her victory.

The huge crowd followed her into the longhouse for dinner.

FLYING through the air in a plane that they would later, while feasting, tell me was a Spitfire, I saw my squad-mates in planes flying in formation with me. My plane's nose began to dip and I saw I was slowly starting to angle downwards and gently descend out of formation. The other pilots gestured emphatically at me, but I couldn't for the life of me tell what they were trying to get me to do.

Pulling on the stick, my nose came up, but the plane started to tilt to the left. The nose kept rising until the engine spluttered and stopped. With the nose still pointed in the air, I saw from the other airplanes that I'd started dropping again. Three of the planes descended after me as I pushed and pulled the stick to try to recover.

Tilting in various directions, I saw the outside world spin, increasingly faster around me, as I was unable to bring the plane under control or restart the engine. Plummeting towards the ground, I saw nothing but water below.

I continued to spin as the ground kept increasing its speed towards me until I crashed, felt a moment of pain, then woke up laying on the ground again.

LOOKING ACROSS THE SUMO RING, I saw a lawyer in a business suit. I might have a chance here I thought, remembering the unarmed combat that I'd been taught over the countless nights of feasting. My opponent touched his fists to the clay. I followed suit and was shocked how quickly he charged and shoved me hard. Flying through the air, I felt myself disintegrate as I crossed the boundary. My last thought was that the warriors were right that you get used to it.

MOVING across the field with our paintball guns, one of my teammates said, "Just up here, you can exit Valhalla and head to the Bifrost." I got excited in anticipation as a hail of gunfire suddenly hit us and I saw paint splatter on my shirt. Recognizing the feeling immediately, I started to disintegrate.

"I JUST CAN'T BELIEVE how much trouble we've been having getting me to the exit," I complained. My nearby companions nodded sympathetically as they chugged mead. "I've died 137 times. It actually might be 138. I've lost count."

"Talk to me when you're in the thousands," one of the lawyers said to me.

"Talk to me when you're in the tens of thousands," one of the knights said to the lawyer.

"Talk to me when you're in the hundreds of thousands," one of the vikings said to the knight.

"Talk to me when you're in the millions," said a Spartan warrior at a nearby table.

"Talk to me when you're in the billions," called a caveman from a few rows over, eliciting cheers and toasts.

"Spell opal," instructed the eight year old.

"O-P-A-L," I instinctively responded.

THUNDERING FORWARD ON MY HORSE, I struggled to keep my lance raised, let alone steady. My opponent was dressed in an academic looking outfit, which made me suspect he was a debater. "Maybe I'll have a chance here," I thought hopefully as his lance caught me on my shield, unseated me, and threw me into the air.

"This could be worse," I thought as I hit the ground, felt the the wind get knocked out of me, and started to disintegrate.

PULLING MYSELF ALONG THE STREET, I heard the heavy footsteps behind me. I thought to myself that it would have been better to end up on the occupier team than the resistance as the soldiers reached and surrounded me.

"Can we talk about this, guys?" I tried as they cut off my slow retreat.

One of the ancient warriors, a Babylonian I'd guess, pushed his spear into my injured legs. Pain shot through me. A French musketeer poked his rapier into my belly, causing me to writhe in agony.

"There's no need to be such assholes guys, come on, you've won," I said. The musketeer jabbed me again, eliciting another howl. A caveman had begun crushing my hand and forearm under repeated blows from his club when a grenade sailed into our group, struck the cobble-stone and killed us all.

"SEM-uh-fohr," the voice said, pronouncing the word carefully and distinctly.

"Could you please use the word in a sentence?" I asked, stalling for time. Glancing left and right I saw an endless line of my fellow competitors stretching out beyond sight on either side of me.

"Mr. Jackson taught the Eagle Scouts semaphore on the camp-out by having them climb hills and then signaling them the day's dinner menu," a disembodied voice said.

"Could you please tell me the word's language of origin?" I asked.

"This word is made up of Greek-derived elements and may have been formed first in French," the voice answered.

I asked, "What is the word's part of speech?"

"Noun," came the response.

"S-E-M-I-F-O-R," I spelled, "semaphore." I felt my body falling apart around me.

TAKING ANOTHER BITE OF CHEESECAKE, I listed the steps for discovery to the lawyer who was drilling me. After success-fully listing them, I said to the table nearby, "Guys, I really need to get to the Bifrost. Are we sure there's no other way for me to get back?"

One of the debaters looked at me thoughtfully. "Well, in THEORY you could exit Valhalla, then make your way there through Asgard. You could follow the stone wall until you

saw the rainbow bridge on the horizon and walk to it from
there. You'd be going the long way around though. We've
been trying to get you as close to the Bifrost as possible,
from Valhalla."

"What?" I said. "I've been here for over a year looking for
a shortcut?"

One of the vikings looked at me seriously, then shrugged
and went back to eating.

"Ok then, next chance we get, just get me back to Asgard
and I'll go the 'long way around' to the Bifrost!" My squad-
mates agreed and the lawyer continued tutoring me.

Looking at my brothers-in-arm over the stone wall, I
thanked them profusely.

One of the vikings stepped forward, "Remember, call us
in your hour of greatest need and we will come to help you.
We look forward to your return, on the glorious day that you
die in battle!"

"Yeah, I'm still not looking forward to that, but thanks
again. I just walk this way," I said, pointing to my left, "until I
see a rainbow bridge in the distance?"

"That should get you there," agreed the debater.

11

Getting up from the couch that had been set up in Zosime's cave, I turned off the 'Game of Thrones' episode as the credits rolled.

"So, explain to me again why microservice architecture is better for web services," Linus asked the dragon.

"A-R-C-H-I-T-E-C-T-U-R-E," I spelled. Everyone, other than the dragon, looked at me in confusion. "She picked up some bad habits in Valhalla," he explained.

"Come on, this is the same thing you've seen throughout the evolution of computer science. Monolithic kernels versus microkernel architecture in operating systems, decentralized computing versus thin clients attached to a server in networking," said Zosime. "Once resources allow it, the flexibility of federation makes sense."

"No more computer talk," said Sari.

Vaeril cut in, "So, you found your way to the Bifrost bridge?"

"Right," I said, continuing the story. "Heimdall and I talked about the Marvel movies. He liked Idris Elba's portrayal. Then he sent me back here."

"Why didn't the dragon or the elf or the ghost go rescue you," asked Sari.

"I knew she didn't need rescuing, princesses are resourceful," said Zosime. "It's strange that the TV show creators changed the story so dramatically from the books. It was obvious where George R. R. Martin was going with them."

"I didn't know where she was or what was happening," said Vaeril. "She wasn't gone that long."

"It was over a year," Sari objected.

"Yes, exactly. Hardly more than a year," the elf agreed. They stroked their pet's chin.

"So, what's your next step?" asked Vaeril.

"I think I have a plan for Kauno," I replied.

FACING THE SHORT, stone wall, Kauno and I looked across it onto the fields of Valhalla. They looked much like the fields of Asgard on our side.

"So, I'll fight all day and feast all night?" the ghost asked. "Will I spend time with other spirits?"

"Constantly," I assured him. "There are countless spirits from every time period. Everyone who died in battle. All the way back to cavemen."

"Eating again sounds nice," the ghost said wistfully. "I'm going to do it," he decided and moved to step across the wall. An eldritch barrier appeared that threw him backwards. The sounds of thunder echoed in the distance, as a storm-front appeared on the horizon.

Flying in formation, a group of five warrior women riding winged stallions circled us and landed gracefully.

Sohvi and four valkyrie who looked like they could be her sisters surrounded us.

"How dare you attempt to violate Valhalla and sully her fields with a spirit who didn't die a warrior's death!" the leader forcefully declared.

"Hi Sohvi," I said and gave her a small wave. "Hi Pegasus, glad you're back in action." The winged stallion regarded me in what might have been a friendly manner.

"Valkyries," I announced. "I don't sully your field with a spirit who didn't die a warrior's death. I return to you a spirit that should have been collected, but has been overlooked by your order."

"This is a grave charge," the leader answered. She examined Kauno. "This is no warrior. He is a victim. Slain by his brother in the bloom of youth. A tragedy, to be sure, but not one fit to battle and feast in Valhalla."

"He was wrestling with his brother when he died. Surely that counts as a death in battle," I suggested.

"Resisting your murder or playing with your brother does not a death in battle make," said the valkyrie leader. "Depart this place and take your victim spirit with you. Perhaps you may yet return if you die on the fields of battle."

"Brothers-in-arms, I call upon you in this my hour of greatest need," I yelled across the wall. "Come and help me fight for justice."

My squad from Valhalla shimmered into place surrounding Kauno, myself and the valkyries. One of the vikings said, "It feels so strange to be outside of Valhalla." A lawyer pointed at the wall and said, "It's right over there." "Yes," acknowledged the viking. "But it still feels weird."

"Brothers and sisters," I yelled to the assembled crew, straining to be heard at the back. "This boy, Kauno, died in battle, fighting his brother. We need to convince these five valkyrie that he died a warrior's death in battle."

The warriors began whispering among themselves. As the discussion became more intense, the vikings, cavemen, and other spirits grew bored with not being taken seriously and wandered over to examine the winged stallions.

A lawyer took the lead and approached the ghost. "Kauno, you're in Asgard, next to Valhalla and surrounded by the divine. On everything here, I want you to swear that you'll be honest with us and answer all our questions truthfully."

"I swear," Kauno said. "And I swear on the goddess Styx as well!"

"That's fine, lad, just fine," said the lawyer. "Now, we all understand it was a traumatic experience, but tell us what happened with you and your brother the day you died."

"Well," he said, "It's like I said before..."

"None of us were there before," said the lawyer. "Start from the beginning."

"My brother and I would get into fights and wrestle, all the time." Kauno said. "I didn't like it, because sometimes he'd take it too far and really hurt me. He wouldn't stop when I begged him to. One time he dislocated my arm and my dad had to pop it back into the socket."

"Abuse doesn't get a spirit into Valhalla," objected the lead valkyrie. "This is a waste of time."

"Please, good lady," said the lawyer. "Our friend here," he gestured to me, "used a once in a lifetime boon for our help in order to try to find out what happened to this young lad. Surely you can spare a few moments to understand and let him tell his story."

"Go on," the valkyrie said curtly.

"Well, the day I died, he had finished off the last pastry

that my mother had made the day before. It was supposed to be mine and I accused him of stealing it. He told me he was strong enough to take it and not to cry like a baby. We started shoving each other and my mother yelled at us to go outside. As we were walking to the door, he shoved me into the stairs leading down to the cellar. I laughed, not realizing how angry he was, and ran down into the cellar and tried to hide from him. He caught up to me and started twisting my arm. I bit him, which made him really angry, then he punched me in the face hard."

"Punches to the face aren't really fair, so that's when I started to get serious and I slapped him. That made him even angrier and he pushed me down and sat on my chest. He pinned my arms at first, and kept slapping my face, but I wiggled my arms loose and tried to get out from underneath him, but he was too strong. The slaps were really hurting, so I punched him in the groin. I know it's dirty fighting, but he was really hurting me."

"And then what happened," the lawyer asked.

"I could barely hit him, I didn't have any leverage, and the angle was all wrong, but it made him so angry. He turned red and started screaming at me. I couldn't even understand what he was saying. I managed to wiggle out from underneath him and started to run for the stairs, when something hit me hard in the head from behind. It hurt so bad. Then he hit me again, and again, and again, and again, and again."

"Eventually the pain stopped and I was standing over the two of us, but I couldn't touch anything. He kept screaming and hitting me with a piece of stone, about the size of your fist. It was all red and my body was a funny angle. My mother eventually came down the stairs to the cellar and she started crying when she saw us."

"I watched my parents raise him until he was an adult, then he left home. My parents moved away a few years after that, then I don't know what happened to them. My friend," he gestured at me, "investigated the town records and..."

The lead valkyrie cut him off. "What happened to your brother or your parents is irrelevant. All we care about is the manner of your death."

"Well, that's my whole story then I guess," said Kauno. "I used to be really angry at my brother and my parents, but now I'm just tired and lonely. I don't want to keep living like this forever."

"This is not a battle," judged the lead valkyrie. "We prohibit your entry to Valhalla."

"Wait, wait, wait," said the lawyer. "I'd like you all to first listen to my little friend here." The eight year old spelling bee participant walked up next to the lawyer.

"Can you give me, as best you remember, the definitions of the word battle?" asked the lawyer.

"I'm really more about spelling than definitions," said the boy. Looking at Kauno he continued, "But I want to help you. I'll do my best."

"One: An encounter between armies, ships, or aircrafts." The valkyries smiled and nodded at this.

"Two: An extended contest, struggle, or controversy," he said, then spelled, "C-O-N-T-R-O-V-E-R-S- Y."

"Please refrain from spelling," instructed the lead valkyrie.

"Sorry ma'am," he said. "Three: A struggle to succeed or survive and Four: a combat between two people."

"So there you have it," said the lawyer. "Based on three of the four definitions of battle, this boy died in battle and deserves his place with us. You can't deny that his wrestling with his brother was an extended struggle. It was a contest as well. It was the very definition of a struggle to survive. He failed, but he fought desperately for life. It was, without a doubt, a combat between two people. Much like the very first battle, between Cain and Abel."

"We do not like these modern notions of battle," announced the leader. "If I had my way, Valhalla would not have any lawyers, debaters, or spelling bee champions."

"I actually never won," corrected the eight year old, earning a glare from the woman.

"I am not convinced," she continued. "But, I will allow my sisters to weigh in. My vote is no."

The second valkyrie looked at the lawyer and sized up Kauno. "I believe you fought the good fight and deserve a place here. I vote yes."

The third valkyrie quickly agreed, "I vote yes."

The fourth valkyrie said, "I agree that modern notions are going too far. My vote is no."

Finally, Sohvi, the fifth valkyrie, said "I have repeatedly insisted to our young friend here that she's a hero, which she keeps denying. If she will be champion to this wretch, I will vote yes if she can draw blood before I do. Will one of my sisters lend her a shield and spear."

Hearing the change in the proceedings, the vikings gathered round us as one of the valkyries who had voted yes gave me her shield and spear. Both were heavier than I was used to and I felt their heft.

All the vikings tried to simultaneously give me advice about the combat, which made all of them incomprehensible. Kauno came close to me and whispered into my ear, "Whatever happens, thanks for trying."

"Perhaps you'll be heading back to Valhalla sooner than you expected, hero," said Sohvi as she started to circle me.

"Maybe your sisters will be taking you to Valhalla on

your shield," I responded, honoring the tradition of pre-combat trash talking. I gave an exploratory lunge with my spear, which was expertly deflected by the warrior woman and prompted an immediate retaliation that I jumped to the right to dodge.

"This is the best court case I've ever seen!" screamed one of the vikings. He joined his companions in howling for my victory, which a few of the non-viking warriors joined in on.

The other four valkyries watched attentively, neither moving nor saying anything.

Sohvi suddenly charged me, giving three quick lunges. I realized they were distractions as I blocked the third attack then had my feet swept out from underneath me by the blunt end of her spear. She jumped in the air, spear pointed downwards to impale me, and landed hard in the spot I'd been in moments before I rolled out of the way and onto my feet.

"Was your incompetence before all an act? How have you suddenly pulled your shit together?" I asked, trying to catch my breath and circling the muscle-bound woman.

"We're on my turf now, pup," said Sohvi. "And speaking of incompetent, who was the one who mistook a ghost for a vampire?"

She lunged forward again, not even breathing heavily yet, and her spear embedded itself in my shield, an inch above where my arm held it. The spear-tip poked through and my arm shook from the impact. With a tug, she pulled her spear back and took my shield with it. I grunted as the shield came off my arm and was taken away from me, skewered by her spear.

"Well, that's that I suppose," she said, looking at me smugly. "Disappointing how quickly you're defeated."

"You haven't scored a hit yet," I insisted, trying to sound

braver than I felt. I twirled my spear menacingly and struck a defensive posture. I gave her a 'come get some' gesture with my, now free, hand.

Suddenly my vision was obscured by a blue, eldritch field. Blinking rapidly, I could see again, and saw that Kauno had run through me and was charging the valkyrie. Dismissively, she swatted at the ghost with her shield arm. The shield passed through him, but when her hand connected, it sent him flying through the air and he disappeared behind the vikings, who roared enthusiastically and watched his flight over their heads.

"Nice try," Sohvi said, as she turned back to me and saw that I had lunged forward, fallen to the ground and had my spearpoint embedded deep into the tip of her left boot. "Humph," she said, dismissively, and lowered her shield and spear.

"Not a very honorable victory," observed the lead valkyrie.

"Honor is the first casualty of war," replied my lawyer.

"Actually, it's truth," corrected one of the debaters, earning him dark looks from our companions.

"I vote yes," said Sohvi. Her four companions began mounting their winged stallions. Walking over to Kauno, she grabbed ahold of the ghost and threw him over the stone wall into Valhalla. His body became corporeal as he flew over the wall and he came down hard on the other side.

Climbing back to his feet, he nursed a clearly broken arm. "What a thing, to have a body again," he called from the other side. "This... hurts! It hurts really bad!" he said enthusiastically. "I'd forgotten what pain feels like."

My comrades started making their goodbyes and drifting back into Valhalla to join him.

Sohvi walked over to me and said, "Good job, hero, but

your spear work sucks. And you need to keep your shield higher." She put her arm around me and drew me close. "Let's get you back to Midgard, Siegfried."

"I'm not Siegfried," I replied with a laugh. The tension of the last half-hour catching up with me and making me laugh longer and louder than I normally would.

"Sure you're not," the valkyrie said. "Just like you aren't a hero."

12

A banner hung in the dragon's cave reading "Happy (BELATED) Birthday!!!" Another, which appeared to be homemade, read, "Congratulations On Getting Into Valhalla!!!" I filled a glass from the punch bowl, and walked over to my father and brother.

"I still can't get over the fact that you died repeatedly in Asgard," my father began again.

"Valhalla," I corrected him. "It wasn't so bad. You get used to it."

"This is my pride. My hubris. What I've put my children through..."

"No, dad," my brother broke in. "It's my fault. I didn't think of the right offer at her birthday last year. If I'd just offered the right deal, all this could have been avoided."

Sheena walked up with three bottles of beer clutched in her hands. "I blame both of you fully and equally," she declared, passing bottles to the two of them. "This is a Finnish craft beer; Linus says it's pretty impressive."

"Really," I reassured them both. "This has been a great

experience so far and I'm looking forward to whatever comes next."

"We've talked it over," my father said. "We both want to transfer ownership of part of our companies to you to resolve the ritual…"

"And I won't accept," I cut him off. "Thanks for coming to my party, but I'm not accepting anything from either of you today. Where's mom?"

My brother gestured to where my mom was in an animated conversation with Mrs. Silverberg.

"I'm going to slip off the other way," I said to the three of them and moved on.

I approached Drigrin, the minotaur, who was talking with some of my squad-mates from Valhalla. "So you're saying, if I structure things that way, there's no way I can get sued?" he asked the lawyer he was getting free legal advice from.

"Anyone can sue you for any reason they want," she explained. The ghosts surrounding them all nodded agreement at this. "This will just put you in the best position to defend yourself if they do."

"Happy birthday," Drigrin said and gave me a hug. "I brought you a present."

"I'm really sorry, but I can't accept. We knew each other before I invoked the ritual, so I'm not allowed to get any assistance from you," I apologized.

"This is ridiculous! I can't do business with you, I can't give you a birthday gift. When is this silly thing going to be over?" he exploded.

"It's frustrating, I know," I said. "But your presence is the best present you could give me. It means a lot to me that you came for my party, thanks!"

Sari and Linus smiled at me as I moved over to greet

them. "Happy birthday!" Linus said and thrust a wrapped box into my hands. "It's a copy of Settlers of Catan," he said, spoiling the surprise. "Maybe we can open it now and play a game with your ghost friends."

"I told you, no board games," said Sari. "And it's her gift, you don't get to open it and play with it."

"But there are so many people here who could play," complained Linus, giving his wife a pleading look.

"I'm sure the ghosts would love to learn how to play and play it with you," I said with a laugh. "And please open my gift for me." I handed the box back to Linus and he smiled at us both.

Some of the Valhalla spirits drifted towards us.

"We tried to think of something to bring you," began one of the World War 2 ghosts. "Since we don't have anything tangible, we thought maybe a little combat training would be good?"

"That would be great, thank you very much," I said. "But not until tomorrow. I don't want everyone to watch me get my ass kicked." The ghosts nodded and wished me happy birthday.

I walked towards Kauno and saw the five valkyrie had arrived and had the finance bros dancing for them without their shirts. Sohvi nodded at me, and I returned her nod. She pointed at a brightly wrapped, large birthday gift on the floor next to them and I gestured thanks to her by holding my hands together and bowing to her.

"Happy birthday," said Kauno who had been talking to Rasmus. Rasmus handed me a present. "It's an embroidered shirt, my wife picked it out, I hope you like it," he explained. "Thank you for sending me a plane ticket to attend your party. I should have brought a costume to fit in better."

"Yes, certainly," I agreed, winking at him. "A costume would help you fit right in."

"Yes," he said emphatically.

"Congratulations on reaching the afterlife," I said to Kauno. "I hope you like it ok."

"It's great! Much better than my life here," the ghost said. "I really can't thank you enough."

"What are friends for," I reassured him and made my excuse to move on.

The elves were talking to another group of Valhalla ghosts, doing their best to stay clustered together while keeping an appropriate distance from one another and talking to non-elves as much as possible. An enormous box was covered by a thin tarp. As I approached, the regent called for everyone's attention.

"We've followed the human custom of celebrating birthdays with a gift," they began. "I can't believe birthdays are celebrated every year. When would you ever get anything else done? But here we are." With a gesture of their hand, Vaeril pulled away the tarp and a man wearing a loincloth was crouched inside.

"Uh, you can't really give people to humans as presents," I said awkwardly. "Really, you shouldn't even be putting him in a cage."

"This is your werewolf," the regent explained. "We hunted him down for you. A non-lethal hunt this time, unfortunately." They put their face to the bars and wagged their finger at the man. "You just give me an excuse, you naughty doggy!"

"He never hurt me, you know," I explained. "Maybe we'd best give him a piece of cake and send him on his way."

"Fine, fine," the regent said, waving dismissively. "Happy birthday from all of us regardless."

A chorus of well-wishes echoed from the assembled elves, many of whom were giving one another dark looks.

"I require you all to stop talking and pay attention," boomed the dragon Zosime. Everyone stopped talking immediately and regarded the large figure that had been looming over the party in his cave. "I did not expect to have this many people visit my cave. Friendship pushes your life in unexpected directions. When I agreed to this party, I thought you all would be slightly more annoying than you have been, so thank you for that."

Hesitant applause greeted this.

"Human birthday's require a small token to demonstrate the giver's admiration. Entry to Valhalla isn't as common a reason for a party, so I didn't get the ghost anything. In my childhood, I had what might be considered a friend. After that ended, I expected not to experience this again for the remainder of my days."

"I think our guest of honor would have made me an excellent captive princess, but it's possible that she's been an even better friend. In light of this, I've signed over interest in a variety of companies, real estate, and commodities. The value is more than the combined value of both of her family's businesses, so this should put an end to the silly ritual. Let us never speak of it again. You are all welcome to enjoy yourselves, while irritating me as little as you possibly can, for the next 45 minutes. After that I expect you to promptly depart."

Moving over to the dragon, I said, 'I'm not sure I can accept that."

Zosime replied, "It's already done and the ritual is complete. Can't you feel it?" I could. He continued. "Thank you for being a friend. I should remind you that I did say we wouldn't talk about it anymore."

"I don't always do what I'm told," I said, with a chuckle. "Even for friends."

ACKNOWLEDGMENTS

Thank you to Dorothy Ryan for editing, beta-reading, and feedback on early versions of this work, to Bryan Caplan for economics information, and my ARC team for getting the word out early.

MESSAGE TO THE READER

Thank you for reading my book. As an indie author, one of the hardest things to match is the high level of proofreading that publishers offer. My abject apologies for the (inevitable) typos, misspellings, or grammatical issues that you might find in this book. Believe it or not, I've proofread this myself repeatedly and had a number of other readers go through it. Remaining errors become increasingly difficult to spot. If you find something, please let me know at john.champaign.writes@gmail.com and I'll make sure to get it fixed for future readers.

AT THE SAME EMAIL ADDRESS, I'm very open to any feedback, questions or ideas.

IF YOU FEEL some gratitude after completing this book, the greatest gift you could give me would be to read something else I've written, more of which will hopefully be coming in the near future. Beyond this, letting any other readers you know who you think would dig this would be greatly appreciated. If you still want to do more (hey, I really like you!), an honest rating and / or review on Amazon or Goodreads would be helpful. One of the hardest things for a new author is trying to connect with readers who would enjoy their work.

I'M NOT TRYING to write to a mass market. My target reader is someone like myself and my close friends. Whoever you are and wherever you're reading this, I'm glad we've been able to connect in this (limited) way.

ABOUT THE AUTHOR

John Champaign is a former university professor and computer programmer who retired at the age of 39 along with his wife Dorothy. He wrote for a popular Canadian personal finance blog for years and also writes non-fiction.

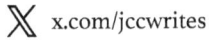 x.com/jccwrites

ALSO BY JOHN CHAMPAIGN

Fiction

Dimensional Traveler: A Deckbuilding LitRPG

Endless Seas: Never Meet Your Idols

Merchant Magician

Non-Fiction

The Gamemaster's Guide To Writing Fiction

Getting Started As A Small Scale Landlord

Negotiating After Getting A Job Offer

The Windmill Method: Buy Real Estate For 15%, 20%, Or More
Below Asking

www.ingramcontent.com/pod-product-compliance
Lightning Source LLC
Chambersburg PA
CBHW052140220626
47052CB00005B/1137